*"You're* ___ *that?"*

Jake sat up, ___ elbows on his knees. . . . "And your martyr act doesn't impress me, though I'll give you high marks for your creative dissembling. Now, suppose you come clean and tell me what you really want with my sister. The loan's paid off, I made sure of that two years ago. . . . And since she's already married, she sure doesn't need the services of some dipsy-doodle wedding consultant . . . never mind that her husband's a drooling idiot who decided he liked being three rather than thirty!"

"I see no reason to further discuss my motives with you, Mr. Donovan," Olivia said. "It's your sister and her husband who were—" she swallowed hard— "victimized."

"Having trouble with the truth?" Jake jeered.

Olivia stood. "I've always accepted the truth . . . that's my problem. If you don't believe me, that's *your* problem. Your sister wanted your opinion, and I can respect that. As for the rest, I'm tired, so—"

. . . "I'll leave, lady, but I'll be back." He raked a cynical, unforgiving eye over the slender woman standing so straight in front of him. "And if you're really after some sort of absolution for your father, it's going to take a lot more than a few humble apologies."

Not trusting his temper any longer, Jake headed for the door. "You better hope your store can manage without you a while, Ms. Sinclair. It might be squeezing blood from a turnip, but I plan to come up with a way to make you pay for what your old man did to my sister and brother-in-law."

**SARA MITCHELL** is the author of five books. In addition to her novel writing, Mitchell has also authored several musical dramas.

## Books by Sara Mitchell

HEARTSONG PRESENTS

HP3—Restore the Joy

# From the Heart

*Sara Mitchell*

*Heartsong Presents*

For Linda, and ten years of friendship blessed by God. Thanks for truly loving me at all times! This one *had* to be for you.

"The master called the servant in, 'You wicked servant,' he said. 'I canceled all that debt of yours because you begged me to. Shouldn't you have had mercy on your fellow servant just as I had on you?' In anger his master turned him over to the jailers . . . until he should pay back all he owed.

" 'This is how my heavenly Father will treat each of you unless you forgive your brother **from your heart**.' "

*Matthew 18:32-35*

ISBN 1-55748-402-3

FROM THE HEART

## one

Soft music, appropriately funereal, floated around the almost deserted room. At the front, in solemn splendor, rested a closed casket draped by a single pall of white carnations. There were no other flowers. Only three seats of the large chapel in the funeral home were occupied.

Sitting in one of the padded chairs was Olivia Sinclair, spine rigid, head bowed. At her side, her mother sat with compressed lips and grim fortitude, biding her time until a polite interval had passed and she, Olivia, and Larry, brother of the deceased, could leave. At the moment, Uncle Harry was looking at the casket, irritation the only emotion registering on his face.

There were no other family members, distant relatives, or friends present to acknowledge the departure of Alton Xavier Sinclair.

Reverend Tucker, the family minister, had spoken a few words some ten minutes earlier, his speech uncharacteristically awkward. In fact, he had agreed to preside over the funeral only because Olivia had gently coerced him, her voice quiet but firm. Apparently not even Reverend Tucker entertained a remote hope that Olivia's father would now be in the presence of the Lord.

Olivia slid a brief look to her mother, whose only words these past interminable hours had been: "Well, I imagine he's finally where everyone wanted him, God forgive me.

But if any man deserves to burn forever, it was your father, Olivia. The only reason we'll attend this farce of a funeral is because your uncle and I need the absolute reassurance that Alton is really dead and can't hurt anybody anymore."

*If only that were true*, Olivia thought now, staring at the coffin. He'd hoodwinked all of them over the years, her father had, with his deceptively charming smile and boyish good looks. First her grandparents, then Uncle Larry . . . then her mother and the three children she'd given him—Olivia, her sister Jennifer, and brother Tom. They were not the only victims, but every person at the bank, too, from the lowliest teller to the wealthiest depositor. Like tares among the wheat, Daddy's bankrupt soul had leeched the life out of everyone around him, leaving a bitter legacy of hatred and revenge. It was somehow fitting that he had died in January, the bleakest, most barren month of the year.

Olivia closed her eyes and tried to pray. The motion was wasted. She could not talk to God with all these feelings seething inside, choking her breath off, and making her skin crawl with nameless dread.

The piped-in music ceased as the funeral director appeared from a side door. With undisguised relief they all stood.

"Let's get out of here," Uncle Larry muttered, practically dragging Alton Sinclair's widow down the aisle. "I need some fresh air, and God knows it will be the first time in over thirty years I'll be able to breathe it easily."

Olivia's last memory of her father was the silent mortician and his assistant wheeling his casket out of the parlor.

After the funeral, struggling with a multitude of tormenting thoughts, she found herself strangely reluctant to return to her store in Barley, a good hour's drive away.

Like thousands of other small southern towns, Barley, North Carolina, enjoyed a serene, slow-moving life-style, comfortably located ten miles off the interstate. Main Street boasted just enough businesses to stay mildly prosperous. There was even a mall on the town's eastern outskirts. Whatever couldn't be had in Barley "twern't worth having," according to the old-timers who daily gathered at the back of Mr. Clarke's seventy-year-old hardware store.

Through her wedding consultant service, The Bridal Bower, Olivia was doing her bit to ensure the town's diversity. She was also enjoying her second full year of operating in the black—for the bittersweet reason that nobody in Barley knew who her father had been. That was about to change, no doubt. The next hours, Olivia suspected, would signal the greatest changes of her life. She had said goodbye to her father, but she was shouldering all the burden of the family name.

". . . and I still can't believe you're actually going through with this," Maria concluded her monologue.

Engrossed in her own thoughts, Olivia had waited patiently throughout the lecture, mouth curved in a half smile, watching her partner and best friend, Maria Santinas, who was still trying to decide if Olivia were teasing or serious. Maria loved to joke about the spaniel-solemn eyes that should have been brown instead of blue-gray, allowing Olivia to tell the funniest joke in the world without cracking a smile.

As a professional wedding consultant, the solemn look had proved useful, and the dry sense of humor had defused many an emotion-laden crisis. Right now, however, Olivia was as serious as she'd been in her entire twenty-six years.

"I'm going to try and atone for Father's cruelty and injustice all these years," she repeated. "One person *can* make a difference, remember?"

"There's one little fact you keep overlooking, kiddo," Maria drawled, pointing a well-chewed pencil at Olivia. "It was your father everyone wanted to tar and feather . . . not you."

Olivia didn't so much as wince. She'd spent the butter part of her life coping with the shame. "I'm still a Sinclair—sins of the fathers and all that. Besides, I'm the only one left. Mom . . . Mom quit caring before I was even born. Tom's in California. And Jennifer married an engineer and moved to Alaska to start a new life—" She paused, furrowing her brow in concentration. "Remember the time Mrs. Duckworth read that Scripture in Sunday school, then pointed to me—'There's *sin* in *Sinclair*,' she said. . . ." Olivia stopped, fighting memories that still rankled years later.

In a reflexive action, she reached for the open daily calendar at the corner of her desk. "Now, I've been planning this for months, ever since Daddy was diagnosed with inoperable cancer last fall." She glanced up. "Don't worry. I'll still manage everything here. At least this is our slowest season."

Maria rolled her eyes. "Knowing your fanaticism for organization, if he'd kicked off in June, I'm sure you could have convinced every last bride in the tri-county area to reschedule for fall." She leaned over Olivia's shoulder, peering at the calendar. "Okay . . . there are no weddings for the next two weeks, and Rollie and I can cover the rest. So what's your plan—a blue-light special on mea culpas, passed along to all parties who've suffered the calculated cruelties of a twentieth-century Ebenezer Scrooge, otherwise known as Alton Sinclair?"

Olivia flushed but met Maria's skepticism without wavering. "Over the past seven years or so, I've compiled a list of sorts, listening to Daddy at the dinner table, reading newspapers, hearing other people talk.... So far, I've got about half a dozen people I plan to see. I know I can't ... atone ... for everything, but I've got to ask their forgiveness at least, see if there's anything I *can* do—" Her voice trailed away. She was suddenly overwhelmed, not only by the impossible nature of the cross she'd chosen to bear, but by the look of sympathy Maria wasn't bothering to conceal. "And I don't need your pity," Olivia mumbled.

Straightening, she picked up her shoulder bag and headed for the back door of the shop. "I have to try, Maria, even if you and Rollie don't like it. I'll touch base with you every Monday morning and Friday afternoon, just as we discussed. Other than that ... see you in three weeks."

"I think," Maria mused aloud, her voice following Olivia out, "that you just might be back here sooner than you planned."

Olivia paused at the back door of the shop, glancing around automatically to make sure everything was in order. She felt inside her purse for the pocket version of the daily calendar on her desk. It was there, in place, and she marched outside without a backward glance.

Jake Donovan paused for a moment, resting against the ropes while he caught his breath, and enjoyed the freedom of dangling two thousand feet up the face of a sheer granite cliff. Far below, the valley floor shimmered and sparkled from the newly fallen snow, while above him a sky blue as an alpine lake stretched toward infinity. The air was so clear and cold it burned his lungs, The only sounds a whistling wind and the single triumphant shriek of a hawk diving toward its kill.

Alone up here, without the stultifying routine found in the rat race most people made of their lives, a man could really find himself. Jake lifted his face, feeling the invigorating bite of the wind . . . and the memory of last night's phone call from his sister intruded as subtly but as dangerously as pending hypothermia. "Ah—" he expressed his frustrations out loud, then finished his ascent. So much for a relaxing week bumming around the Rockies before his next job!

Four hours later, he was back on the ground, swiftly and efficiently breaking camp. In four more hours, he was at Stapleton Airport, Denver, boarding a plane for the first leg of his flight to Charlotte, North Carolina. Beth would be waiting at the airport, her drawn, care-worn face looking far older than its thirty years, brown eyes dulled by permanent fatigue.

What was wrong now?

She'd sounded so strange over the phone, almost—Jake searched his mind for a word, waving aside the hovering flight attendant who couldn't understand why he wouldn't eat the plastic meal she was offering—incredulous. That was the word he was looking for! Like his sister had just taken a fist in her stomach. No . . . that wasn't it, either. Beth hadn't sounded like she was upset or in pain, and she had promised Jake that nothing had changed for the worse with Davy. She just needed to talk something over with her big brother. No matter that *she* was the stable nine-to-fiver and Jake the proverbial rolling stone.

He leaned back in the seat, forcing his body to relax. All his life he'd taken care of his sister. She was the only responsibility he'd ever accepted without question, no strings attached. Whether he was tramping through a jungle in South America or biking through the Alps, all Beth had to do was call.

Ignoring the droning voices, the constant noise, the irritation of being confined, Jake closed his eyes and switched off. He had a feeling he was going to need all the rest he could manage. At least, for the next few hours, he didn't have to worry about insects or frostbite.

Beth hugged him tightly, but avoided his gaze.

"I'll drive, you talk . . . but wait until we're out of the airport," he ordered, tossing his bag in back and gently bullying her into the passenger seat of the beat-up Ford she'd been driving for the last eight years. Jake hated the car, but sometimes Beth could dig in her heels more firmly than he. The last time he'd bought her a car, Beth signed it over to some penniless widow down the street.

Night was approaching rapidly. Jake turned on the lights and fiddled with the heater. After Colorado, forty degrees seemed like summertime, but Beth was shivering. He maneuvered the vehicle out of the airport and headed southwest, toward the little North Carolina town where Beth and Davy lived. Now, of course, only Beth lived there.

Jake glowered at the bleak countryside, thinking his sister looked as gray and lifeless as the waning February day. "You said Davy's the same, right?"

Beth nodded. "I wouldn't lie to you about that."

She had married Davy when both kids were fresh out of the vocational tech school. Scrupulously saving, working sixteen-hour days, within three years they'd accumulated enough money to take out a loan for Davy to open his own small engine repair shop. Then—

"Talk," Jake said tersely, giving the road part of his attention while honing in on every nuance of Beth's subdued recital.

"Three days ago this . . . young woman came to see me," she began. Jake felt her staring at him, hesitating. He forced himself to wait, knowing Beth would clam up if he pushed too hard. "Her name was Olivia . . . Sinclair."

At that, Jake almost swerved off the road. *"What?"*

In the dim interior of the car, her faint smile was barely discernible. "I had the same reaction."

"You don't have to say another word," Jake said from between clenched teeth. "I'll handle this now, sis. You just tell me where the little—"

"Wait a minute, big brother, before you go all aggressive and protective on me—" Beth patted his shoulder. "Not, of course, that I don't need that, with Davy—" Her voice wobbled, but she rallied like she always did. "She looks so *nice*, Jake, it completely threw me for a loop. I was on my lunch hour, and she asked if she could join me. You wouldn't believe how hesitant, almost afraid she sounded."

Jake mumbled something to himself and Beth apologized. "Sorry. I know I'm rambling and you hate that. I'm trying to explain, but I still have so much trouble—"

"Just tell me what she demanded. Obviously, she's dear

old Dad's new hatchet-man. Sorry. . .*person* . . .and—"

"I'm going to tape your mouth shut, Jake Donovan."

Jake rotated his shoulders, and took a deep breath. For a few moments neither of them spoke. As always, he appreciated his sister's ability to bring him up short, then back off without harping on his regrettable temper. "I'm okay now," he promised, reaching one arm across in a brief hug. "No more interruptions, or promises as to how I plan to wipe my boots on Ms. Sinclair and her jerk of a father."

"Her father's dead."

This time he managed to keep the car firmly in the road. "Good riddance."

Beth actually chuckled. "Yeah, well, that's what this is apparently all about. His daughter wants—in her words—'to try and atone for some of my father's injustices.' She's been looking up some of us pathetic hard-luck stories and is begging for a chance to help."

"And pigs fly!" Jake shot back. "I'll have to hand it to her . . . the lady's got a unique approach, a lot more subtle than her old man's. I'm glad you called, mouse. You're much too soft and sweet to take on a female Attila the Hun." He grinned into the night, his thoughts churning. "But as well you know, I'm *not*."

# two

*I don't know how much more of this I can take*, Olivia thought, hands clutched tightly together in her lap. Yet she continued to sit quietly in her discreet suit, hair carefully arranged, face a serene mask. She had no choice. Quitting was *not* an option.

Head high, she allowed the contempt and vitriolic spate of words to wash over her, through her, each word a stinging verbal blow.

"... and, young lady, I hope you're as humiliated and hurt as I was six years ago," Samuel MacKenzie concluded, leaning back in his massive desk chair and studying Olivia with satisfaction. "Yep, I trust you're squirming, like I squirmed when your excuse for a father refused to extend my loan two lousy weeks, smiling like a shark and looking at me as if I were dockyard scum."

"I'm aware—very painfully aware—that I can't undo the past, Mr. MacKenzie." Olivia knew she sounded too mechanical, but then the powerful businessman was the sixth such encounter. At least, she *could* finally make it through what she'd dubbed her "abasement spiel" without sounding like a cowed puppy. "As I told you when you agreed to see me, I only wanted to—to say I'm sorry and—and—" This was the hardest part, especially since thus far she'd encountered nothing but disbelief and flat rejection. Her voice hoarsened to a near whisper. "I wanted to ask, as a Sinclair, if you could possibly forgive what my father

14

did to you."

Samuel MacKenzie snorted. "Give me a break. You one of those religious fanatics or something?" He shook his head. "You got grit, I'll give you that. Don't know another soul with the brass-bound gall to sit across from me and spout off that kind of drivel." He leaned forward, removing his glasses, and peered intently into Olivia's face. "Tell me, Ms. Sinclair, just how far would you go to secure forgiveness, as you say? Can you make financial reparations? Spend the next seven years or so in bondage to the various folks your father ground under his boot?"

The hot color crept relentlessly up her cheeks. "If I could, I would. Even though that's not possible, I just wanted—needed—to see if there was any way I could clear the Sinclair name. What my father did—" She stopped, biting her lip.

"—you can't undo. Yes, Ms. Sinclair, you've already acknowledged that regrettable fact." Mr. MacKenzie stood and walked around his desk. The hard, booming voice softened a little, sounding so kind now that Olivia's eyes began to water. "But like I told you—you got grit, and I admire that. So I'll give you some free advice, which we both know is more than your old man would have done—"

He paused, then snagged a tissue from the box on his desk and matter-of-factly handed it to Olivia. As if in a dream, she accepted it and dabbed her eyes.

"You can see," Mr. MacKenzie continued, making a sweeping gesture around the plush office, "that I'm fairly successful in spite of your father. He might have controlled a lot of money and owned the largest bank in the area, but he didn't own the entire state of North Carolina.

I got another loan elsewhere and paid him off. Then I moved here to Statesville and haven't looked back. My point is this: There are lots of ways to fight the battles in your life, including knowing when it's time to withdraw. Believe me, Ms. Sinclair, you can't win this one!"

Olivia wadded the tissue into a tight little ball. "Maybe not," she conceded, her voice shorn of emotion. "But I have to try.... I—I just can't live with the name any longer if I don't make an effort. If I find even one person who'll forgive what my father did, this whole thing will have been worth it."

The busy executive, whose secretary had warned Olivia he had the manners of a pit bull when annoyed, reached out and gently captured Olivia's small fist inside his big hand. "I don't hold much truck with do-gooder Christians gushing over God's love and forgiveness. They preach a good sermon on Sundays, then doublecross with the best con artists in the land on Monday. Of course, never in my fifty-nine years have I met a Christian quite like you." He dropped her hand and walked back around his desk.

"Since it means so much to you . . . okay. I'll forgive your old man. As it turns out, he probably did me a favor in the long run anyway. Now get out of here and let me get back to work. You've wasted enough of my valuable time—not to mention your own."

Olivia plodded down the sidewalk in a daze, clutching her coat against a raw February wind. She still couldn't believe what had happened, couldn't absorb the fact that, after two endless weeks of rejection and ridicule, someone had actually granted her wish.

Strangely enough, she didn't feel one whit better.

Shoulders slumped, muscles aching from the strain of projecting an attitude of calm determination, Olivia waited at the corner. When the light flashed to green, she stepped off the curb without looking.

"Watch it, lady!"

Hands yanked her backward as a small car careened by, missing Olivia by barely a yard.

"Wow, that was close! You all right, ma'am?"

She looked up into the concerned face of a gangling teenage boy. "Thanks. I guess I should have been looking."

He grinned. "And they say *teenagers* are dangerous drivers! The lady driving that car looked old enough to be my grandmother."

Olivia managed to smile back. "Well, thanks again. I'll be more careful in the future, and I'll tell all my friends with teenage sons to cut them some slack."

Statesville was less than an hour's drive from Barley. Since it was only a little past four, Olivia decided to stop by The Bower. Maria and their tireless assistant, Rollie Jones, had thus far kept things going without a hitch, largely because Olivia had everything so meticulously organized that even a twelve year old could have managed.

Bone-deep weariness engulfed her, though she knew it was more exhaustion of spirit than body. She needed to do something, prove she wasn't an ugly worm in need of burial in the back garden. She needed . . . affirmation.

The Bridal Bower occupied the former site of a seconds fabric store, two blocks off Main. Olivia parked out front, then just sat there for a few minutes, basking in the tangible evidence of her success in at least one area of her life.

A hand-painted tangle of vines and flowers twined over the front door. Coordinating displays in the bay windows on either side advertised the various services offered by The Bower, from engraved invitations to catered receptions. A triangular sticker below the store's logo announced Olivia's membership in the Association of Bridal Consultants. Next to that was a fish-shaped sticker quietly proclaiming the store's Christian viewpoint.

Everyone—including and especially her father—had predicted her venture would go belly-up like the fabric store. At the thought, fresh tears stung Olivia's eyes. She grabbed her purse and went inside.

Maria, looking frazzled, was talking with two women, probably mother and daughter. They were sitting in the store's get-acquainted alcove, which meant this was an initial visit. Comfortably padded chairs were clustered around a large table holding brochures describing all the services available.

When Maria caught sight of Olivia, her chocolate-brown eyes widened in relief. "Ah, here's Ms. Sinclair now. Maybe she can better explain Bridal Bower's policies—" Gracefully vacating her chair, Maria made way for Olivia and shot her an apologetic smile. Olivia suppressed a sigh. Even after five years and a reputation rapidly encompassing the entire state, their maverick policies still sometimes generated consternation.

"This is Janine Careyton and her mother, Vanessa," Maria said. "They haven't quite agreed on—"

"—on much of anything," finished Janine, her voice a shade away from outright anger.

"I won't have people accusing me of scrimping on my

daughter's wedding. I have already explained that money is *not* an issue." Dripping with jewelry, hair fresh from a salon, Mrs. Careyton eyed both Olivia and Maria as if they were indentured servants.

Olivia was not unfamiliar with the look. She glanced at the younger woman, sensing immediately that her mother's words had pushed Janine over the edge.

"Mother, you *know* how Father feels, especially after the two of you went into debt when Belinda got married. If you recall, you almost divorced over it. Which—" she added nastily—"is exactly what Belinda and Mike did less than two years after you dumped twenty thousand dollars into their grand society wedding!"

Her mother's lips clamped shut and she darted her daughter a frigid look of displeasure.

Olivia decided it was time to intervene. "May I say something?" She kept her voice deferential but firm enough to command attention. Sitting with arms relaxed at her sides, leaning back in a nonaggressive pose, she waited until both women nodded.

Then she leaned forward slightly. "I have a feeling, Mrs. Careyton, that you still might not understand some of the basic philosophies we hold to here at The Bridal Bower."

"Oh, I did, and that's why—"

"Your assistant has shared that information," Vanessa Careyton's imperious voice overrode her daughter's.

Olivia inclined her head. "Including our promise to defer primarily to the *bride's* wishes, unless she specifies otherwise in writing?"

Two spots of color appeared on the older woman's thin, aristocratic face. "Madam, if I choose to hire you as my daughter's consultant, I will be paying the fees—and you will do as I suggest, or we'll find another consultant."

Olivia stood. "I understand. In that case, I don't think The Bridal Bower will be able to provide the quality of service you desire." She kept her face expressionless while mother and daughter swept out, the daughter with one last anguished backward look.

Maria came to stand beside Olivia, shaking her head. "Whew! Am I glad you stopped by. That woman could intimidate a dragon. I was sweating and stuttering like some blithering idiot." She grinned. "*You* sit there, calm and collected as a nun, then manage to get rid of them in less than five minutes. Which is why you're the boss, right?"

"Well . . . we learn the hard way."

"Ain't it the truth? Remember—" She stopped, then tilted her head to observe Olivia. "You look whacked. No luck today either?"

"I don't know." Olivia restacked the skewed piles of brochures on the table, aligned pads and pencils. She didn't look at Maria. "The last person I talked to was a Samuel MacKenzie. He's this huge grizzly of a man, a contractor, and, like everyone else, he spent the first ten minutes heaping abuse upon my head."

"Olivia—"

"But then he—he actually patted my hand . . . and agreed to forgive my father." She still couldn't believe it. "That's the first time it's happened, but Maria . . . I just feel empty." She swallowed the lump crowding her throat. "I don't understand . . . when this means so much to me."

Maria hugged her. "You can't force the issue, honey. You're sweet and compassionate and determined, but unfortunately your papa was heartless and cruel. Most people aren't going to forget—much less forgive—no matter how nice you are. We've tried to tell you that, but you just refuse to listen. Stubborn as garlic breath you are."

"Thanks a lot." Olivia rubbed her temples. "I knew I could depend on my best friend and partner to give me a boost, salve my tattered self-esteem." When Maria looked stricken, Olivia managed to summon up a flicker of a smile. "I'm teasing, sort of, okay? Just ignore me. I'm going to work a few hours here and go home. So ... didn't you tell me Barbara Drake finally settled on her colors? What about her gown?"

Looking relieved, Maria nodded. "No gown yet. Blue and cream for the colors. Rollie's out canvassing now— oh!" She smacked her head. "I forgot! Some guy stopped by, wanting to see you about some business matter, not a wedding, 'cause he said he wasn't engaged. He's a friend of Noel Chambers ... you know, we did that wedding last August? Anyway, you should have seen this dude! If Rick and I weren't tying the knot, I'd have flirted like the dickens. His eyes—"

"What did he want, Maria?"

"—were this piercing gray and the way he looked at me made my knees weak. And his voice—"

"Maria!"

"Oh, all right. It was worth a try, anyway." She slanted Olivia a look of exasperation. "You're such a contradiction, friend—running a business to ensure happily-ever-afters to everyone else, but never making any effort to ensure your own."

Olivia gave a menacing gesture. "One more word and I'll stuff a sample book down your throat."

Maria laughed. "Sure you will! You're about as tough as a day-old kitten. That man now—okay, okay." She held up her hands, fending off Olivia's. Abruptly the playfulness ended. "I—um—hope you don't mind . . . I gave him your home address and phone number since he asked for you by name and knows the Chambers family. There. Now you have a good reason to choke me."

Stunned, Olivia licked suddenly dry lips. "I don't believe it. You *know* our policy, and the reason . . . and you gave the info anyway?"

"Well . . . I didn't mean to." Maria gave her a hangdog look. "I do know better, but he had a way about him, and before I realized it. . . . Anyway, I'm sure he's not a serial killer or something, but I did want to warn you. Forgive me?"

Olivia winced. "Don't be a goose. Of course I forgive you. But I sure hope this doesn't turn out to be more trouble."

# three

Drumming his fingers on the steering wheel, Jake scanned the quiet tree-lined street, blurred now with evening shadows. Just his luck Ms. Sinclair was working late, probably gouging some gullible, starry-eyed bride-to-be. A professional wedding consultant. Now *there* was a racket. Obviously Alton Sinclair had been only too happy to loan—or *donate*—a bundle to his daughter so she could have her own profitable business.

Jake shifted irritably in the seat, unable to erase the contrast from his mind—Beth in her worn, unfashionable skirt and blouse, juggling two jobs and living in a run-down duplex, and this chic boutique with the well-dressed assistant he'd met earlier. If Olivia Sinclair treated him in the same sophisticated, smarmy manner, well . . . he just hoped he could refrain from throttling the conniving female when he laid eyes on her.

The rules of whatever game Ms. Sinclair was playing were about to change, Jake thought, his gaze moving to the tiny house across the street. A boxy, one-story oddity sandwiched between two Victorian relics, the drab little house made Jake positively claustrophobic. It also made him uneasy, since that was where Olivia Sinclair was supposed to live. He wondered—not for the first time—if Olivia's friendly assistant had pulled a fast one on him.

More likely she lived in one of those pretentious Victorian houses, and he owed the charming Maria a return visit. The thought that two women might be stringing him along as if he were some gullible yahoo made Jake's blood boil.

A car turned into the driveway and he sat up, watching the woman driver alight. Mentally he ticked off her description—average height and shape, straight darkish hair just brushing her shoulders, wearing a snappy suit that shouted money and style. Yep, that must be the barracuda herself. And she was headed for the shabby cottage, pulling keys from her purse. Something didn't add up here, but Jake didn't waste more time in speculation.

He loped across the street, catching her halfway up the weed-infested path leading to her front door. "Olivia Sinclair?" She jerked around, looking both startled and resigned.

"Sorry," Jake apologized, not meaning it. "I thought your assistant would have told you I'd be waiting. My name's Jake Donovan."

"I—she did mention you, but I'm afraid I'll have to ask you to come to the store during office hours, Mr. Donovan. I don't conduct business from my home."

His gaze slid to the house, then back to Olivia's face. "Not surprising," he murmured. Even though it was almost dark, he could see a fiery blush sweep up her cheeks. Interesting. He wouldn't have thought a female like her still knew how to blush.

"Excuse me." She was trying to brush him off, turning her back to march on up the path.

Jake ground his teeth. "I'm not interested in being suckered into your fancy wedding consultant set-up," he called, pitching his voice just loud enough to reach her ears. "But we do have some business to discuss, Ms. Sinclair, and since I have plans tomorrow, right now's the best time for *me*." He joined her at the door and deftly lifted the keys from her hand. "Shall we go inside . . . or do you want this stuffy, southern-wealth neighborhood to hear what I think of the contemptible Alton Sinclair and his equally contemptible daughter?"

A quiver rippled through her, but other than that, Ms. Sinclair didn't respond a lick to his deliberate goading. Then, "Are you sure this can't wait until tomorrow?"

A cool customer, Jake surmised, doubtless accustomed to hearing a lot worse, if her reaction was anything to go by. Well, he'd be only too happy to oblige. "Not a chance." He unlocked the door, then gestured for her to enter.

"Come in," Olivia offered, her voice so dry Jake shot her a speculative look.

"Thank you," he returned, mimicking her tone.

She led the way through a dark entry hall, turning on lights. "Would you like something to drink—tea, cola—or would you prefer to start attacking my character immediately?"

The back of Jake's neck tingled, a bad sign. He eyed the contained, eerily calm woman standing in a pool of lamplight, looking for all the world as if she'd just asked his opinion of the weather. Ms. Sinclair wasn't showing a shred of emotion. Being a shrewd observer of human nature, Jake knew such behavior was unnatural—and thereby must be a calculated pose. What was her game? "I could use some coffee," he said, watching her closely. Olivia Sinclair wasn't what he'd expected, and Jake didn't like it.

"Have a seat. I'll be right back."

After she disappeared through a doorway, Jake prowled the tiny living room, searching for clues, for signs of vulnerability. His uneasiness grew. While Ms. Sinclair definitely had a flair for color and decoration, there was little evidence of the same prosperity he'd seen at her store. In fact, her furniture looked almost as shabby as Beth's.

Sitting down on a sagging, faded green couch, Jake tossed a tapestry throw pillow back and forth while he chewed over what to make of the woman in the kitchen.

She returned several moments later bearing a tray complete with cream, sugar, and two steaming mugs. Blue-gray eyes, large and uncertain, regarded Jake without blinking. He was beginning to feel like a complete jerk, but he suppressed the guilt.

"What did my father do to you?" she asked tonelessly, correctly assessing the reason for his visit.

*This* subdued woman was really Sinclair's daughter? Jake took a mug, ignoring the milk and sugar, then sprawled back against the couch. "My sister, Beth Carmichael, happens to be married to one of your father's many victims." He paused, waiting.

Comprehension lit the pale, carefully expressionless face. "I visited your sister a week ago and heard about her husband." Olivia stared across at Jake. "I know you won't believe me, but I hadn't known until then what had happened to him." She wrapped both hands about her own mug, as if to warm them. "I guess she called you after my visit?"

"Yeah. I'm all she's got, now that Davy's a permanent mental case and ward of the state—all courtesy of your charming father. Now you waltz in three years after the fact, thinking that a simple apology can wipe the slate clean?" Raw anger, still too near the surface, licked through his words. *Not smart, Donovan.* Jake took a couple of deep breaths, reluctantly admiring Olivia Sinclair's tremendous control. Or was it indifference?

"I know it doesn't sound like much—"

"You're mighty right about that!"

"—but I have to try." Abruptly, she set the mug down and

leaned back in her chair, closing her eyes.   The calm, competent professional metamorphosed to a haggard young woman who looked totally exhausted. "Can you possibly understand how it feels, knowing what my father was, having to live with his reputation . . . always wondering what everyone is saying behind my back?" She opened her eyes, gazing blindly over his shoulder. "I'd give anything to make it all right, fix the wrongs. But at least I can tell people I'm sorry. I need—" She clamped her mouth shut, so tight her lips turned white.

Irrationally, he found this first evidence of vulnerability angering him more than her seeming indifference. "You're sort of pathetic, lady, you know that?" Jake sat up, leaning his elbows on his knees, ruthlessly imposing Beth's drawn face over Olivia   Sinclair's. "And your martyr act doesn't impress me, though I'll give you high marks for your creative dissembling. Now, suppose you come clean and tell me what you really want with my sister. The loan's paid off, I made sure of that two years ago. There's not a chance you can talk her into even setting foot inside Fidelity Bank. And since she's already married, she sure doesn't need the services of some dipsy-doodle wedding consultant . . . never mind that her husband's a drooling idiot who decided he liked being three rather than thirty!"

"I see no reason to discuss my motives further with you, Mr. Donovan," Olivia said. "It's your sister and her husband who were—" she swallowed hard—"victimized."

"Having trouble with the truth?" Jake jeered.

Olivia stood. "I've always accepted the truth . . . that's my problem. If you don't believe me, that's *your* problem. Your sister wanted your opinion, and I can respect that. As for the rest, I'm tired, so—"

Jake stood as well, drained his mug, then set it down on the tray. "I'll leave, lady, but I'll be back." He raked a cynical, unforgiving eye over the slender woman standing so straight in front of him. "And if you're really after some sort of absolution for your father, it's going to take a lot more than a few humble apologies."

Not trusting his temper any longer, Jake headed for the door. "You better hope your store can manage without you a while, Ms. Sinclair. It might be squeezing blood from a turnip, but I intend to come up with a way to make you pay for what your old man did to my sister and brother-in-law."

In the hall on the way out was a desk with a daily-planner notebook on top. Jake stopped, flicked contemptuously through several pages, then slammed it shut and opened the front door. "Program me into your busy life, Ms. Sinclair. And you can tell your sweet little assistant she'll have to con brides on her own for a while. *You're* going to be doing some real work for a change."

Olivia sat motionless after Jake Donovan left, too numb to do anything else. Earning forgiveness, she was learning, consisted of endless, exhausting lessons in humility. And after the brutal confrontation with Jake Donovan, she couldn't help wondering if she were about to reap a whirlwind of emotional destruction far more devastating than her father's lifelong cruelty.

Late that night, as on most nights, she fell asleep asking the Lord for help with the intolerable burden . . . and waiting in vain for comfort.

## *four*

"Morning!" Rollie opened the back door with her ample hip, sending cold air and rain blowing across the room. Balanced in her arms were several thumbed-through issues of the latest bridal magazines, which she promptly dumped onto her own desk. "Didn't expect to find you here today, especially this early."

Olivia finished rescuing several blown papers. After a restless night, she'd escaped to the shop practically at daybreak to work on the account books. Shrugging her shoulders to rid them of kinks, Olivia wondered if there was any use in asking her blunt, worldly-wise assistant about yesterday's encounter with Jake Donovan.

Rollie Jones looked like a plump, cherubic grandmother who loved to knit sweaters and rock on the front porch. In reality, she possessed the energy of a four-year-old boy and could also inveigle the stripes off a tiger if she chose. After pouring a cup of coffee, she returned to prop a hefty hip on the corner of Olivia's desk. "What is it, honey? We both know there's nothing wrong with The Bower's financial solvency."

Olivia smiled briefly, toying with her pencil. In four years, Rollie had come to know her too well. "Did Maria tell you about the man who stopped by here yesterday, asking for me?"

"The 'good-looking macho dude' who charmed her into giving out your address and phone number?" Eyebrows raised, Rollie surveyed Olivia over the rim of her mug. "Maria needs to watch that mouth of hers. I gather the gentleman did pay you a visit."

"You might say that," Olivia said, remembering the silky promise woven through Jake Donovan's parting words. "And . . . it *is* because of Daddy—not anything concerning The Bower."

The cherubic features hardened with censure. "Maria and I warned you that this notion of yours was asking for trouble. I still can't believe your mother let you—"

"I'm almost twenty-seven, Rollie, not seventeen. Besides, Mom doesn't know. I haven't spoken to her since the funeral. Right afterward, she flew off to the Virgin Islands for a month." Staring at the neat columns of figures on the desk in front of her, Olivia couldn't help wondering if her mother's brand of therapy was, in the long run, far more effective than her own.

"Mmph." Rollie came around and wrapped a comforting arm about Olivia, giving her a hard hug. "I'm thinking a long vacation might not be such a bad idea for you, too. Now . . . before Maria blows in, and I have to go pick up the Bibles from the bookstore—eight this time, right?— tell me about this man."

Tell her about Jake Donovan. Olivia studied the middle-aged woman who had been widowed over half her life. Her unsentimental doctrine—"You made the bed, honey, so don't fuss about the dirty sheets—" consisted more of judgment than mercy.

She and Jake Donovan would make a good team, Olivia thought, even if Rollie was a charter member of Barley Presbyterian, and Jake . . . well, Olivia suspected the man would as soon swallow a snake as darken the doors of a church—any church.

"I'm waiting—"

Olivia walked over to the waist-high table where silk flowers, fabric samples of bridesmaids' gowns, and dozens of pictures littered the surface. Maria's enthusiasm for work never had included a sense of order. Olivia began tidying things up while she talked, not looking at Rollie. "Last week I visited a couple who took out a loan at Daddy's bank almost four years ago. The terms were—" she had to take a catch-breath—"outrageous. They couldn't make the payments, of course, and the bank foreclosed."

"Sounds typical," Rollie observed, voice matter-of-fact, as she helped Olivia straighten the table.

Olivia smiled mirthlessly. "Don't remind me. Only this time, the man couldn't cope with his failure. Dave Carmichael just gave up on life, his wife told me. I gathered he was always sensitive and introverted. Eventually he got so bad he wouldn't even eat, and she finally had to have him committed to a mental hospital. She's been told he might never come out of it."

"Olivia—"

"They'd only been married four years." Even now the shame and horror was overwhelming. She gripped the edge of the table, struggling to keep her voice even. "Now his wife works two jobs and eighteen-hour days to pay for his care."

"God have mercy," Rollie muttered reverently. "Poor soul." Then she crossed her arms over her chest. "But don't do this to yourself, Olivia. What happened to him— to all these people—it's not your fault. You've got to accept that. Just give the past, and your father, over to God."

"I can't." She shook her head, and the words spilled out in a torrent. "I've tried for years, and I can't. I used to beg Mom to do something . . . then my brother and sister. Even Uncle Larry. But they'd all given up and just didn't care anymore. Nothing was going to change Daddy, they said." She dashed an angry hand across her eyes. "So, I have to do *something*, anything, and when Jake Donovan comes around again, looking for me, I plan to do whatever he demands, see if *that* will make a difference. It didn't help when Mr. MacKenzie forgave Daddy—did I tell you? I still feel guilty and so full of this horrible *shame* that sometimes I think I'll go insane."

Neatly stacked behind them were the gift Bibles already engraved with the newlyweds' names. Olivia grabbed one and thrust it in Rollie's face. "*This* is why I have to do something. It's too late for Daddy, okay, I accept that. But I need the forgiveness. I need to—to try and somehow erase the sins of my father, like Jesus erases our sins." She lifted a hand to forestall Rollie's response. "So don't lecture me anymore about my 'scheme,' okay? I've made up my mind. For two weeks I've been begging people's forgiveness and, you're right, it hasn't worked. So I'll try Jake Donovan's plan . . . whatever it is."

He strolled into the store two hours later, while Maria was helping six chattering bridesmaids in one alcove, and Olivia sat in another with an engaged couple, helping them decide on wedding invitations. "Finish looking through this book," she suggested to Janet and Mark, "and if you'll excuse me just a minute—"

Mouth dry, heart skittering like a pair of frightened mice, Olivia slowly made her way over to Jake Donovan.

He watched her approach through metallic pewter eyes as if contemplating where to make the first strike. Or, Olivia thought half-hysterically, maybe it was more like speculating how he planned to carve her up and use her for fish bait. He looked big and tough, dark hair tousled, his gray eyes cold as the February day. Olivia wanted to crawl under the nearest table.

"Busy morning," he greeted her blandly enough, his gaze raking the shop and its clients.

"Yes. Are—are you going to make a scene?" She knew the potential existed. Tension radiated from every pore of the tightly coiled, powerful body.

His penetrating eyes zeroed in on her. He frowned. "What would you do if I did . . . um . . . 'make a scene?' "

Breath wedged in her throat, Olivia clasped her hands behind her back so he couldn't see her anxiety. "If I couldn't persuade you to leave, Maria would phone the police."

"I could do you—and this place—a lot of damage before the police could arrive, and be miles away without a trace." He paused, adding roughly, "Quit looking like that. Regardless of what you think, I'm not a wanton criminal or a heartless rogue like your old man. Besides, the idea here is to allow you the opportunity to grovel, isn't it? Work out some manner of penance to absolve you from responsibility for what happened to my sister and brother-in-law?" He smiled suddenly over her head at Maria and waved, looking so friendly and approachable that Olivia almost gasped. "Your assistant is palpitating with curiosity, Ms. Sinclair. Shall we join them, and you can explain the situation—" He arched one slashing brow. "Or can I interest you in a cup of coffee somewhere more private?"

"Nobody else here deserves having their joy, their dreams crushed, Mr. Donovan. If you'll give me another thirty minutes, I'd be more than willing to hear what you have to say." She glanced back toward an oblivious Janet and Mark, happily poring over the style sample catalogs. "Right now I'm trying to help a young couple save as much money as possible so they don't start out married life head over heels in debt."

She tilted her head, watching him. "I know. Not in character for a Sinclair, is it? Don't worry, I'm sure you'll discover all my other flaws soon enough." In spite of her discipline, Olivia's voice shook on the last words, the sting of shame heating her cheeks.

Incredibly, Jake Donovan's hand lifted, the fingers skimming Olivia's hot cheek almost like a caress. "Every single one," he agreed softly. For a paralyzing second their gazes held. "Thirty minutes," he repeated. "I'll be waiting outside."

He left, the melodic door chimes ringing out its "Here Comes the Bride" melody in his wake. The absurdity would have made Olivia smile, except that her cheek was still burning from the light brush of the man's fingers. And for the next twenty minutes, she found her own hand creeping up to touch the spot.

Janet and Mark finally left, relieved to have found almost exactly what they wanted for a fraction of the price they'd been prepared to pay. "Remember," Olivia counseled as she walked them to the door, "marriage is supposed to be forever, so you need to commit yourself to a life of joy—not debt."

"Thanks, Olivia." Janet embraced her impulsively.

"You're the greatest! I'm so glad we found The Bridal Bower. Thanks to you, our wedding is going to be the most wonderful event of my entire life!"

Olivia watched them walk down the street, arms entwined, heads close together, talking and laughing. The rain had ended an hour earlier, with a weak but welcome sun breaking through the clouds, warming the day. *I'll never have what they have, will I, Lord?*

Lifting her head, Olivia slowly turned toward Jake Donovan. Leaning against a lamppost, arms crossed and wearing a worn leather jacket and aviator sunglasses, he looked about as approachable as a Doberman.

Shouldering himself away from the post, he sauntered toward Olivia. "Touching," he observed, eyebrow lifted in another ironic arc toward the departing couple. "And to think I'm about to deprive you of more opportunities to arrange wonderful events for gullible young men and naïve little girls with stars in their eyes."

"I'm not what you think I am," Olivia began, then shook her head. "Never mind—it doesn't matter. I am a Sinclair, which makes people like you blind to everything else. Let me fetch my coat, and I'll be back."

Maria slipped through the crowd of young women and hurried over. "Are you sure you know what you're doing?" she whispered, brown eyes filled with worry. "He was so nice yesterday. . . . I still can't believe any of this. Are you *sure*?"

"No." Olivia tugged on her raincoat. "I just know I have to see what he wants, and agree if at all possible. I can't live like this anymore, Maria. I can't."

Maria lifted her hands. "Then be careful. I know you, Olivia. Don't let him chew you up and spit you out, hoping you'll feel better.  Life doesn't work that way."

"He can't chew me up and spit me out—" Olivia tied the belt of her raincoat, checked her purse for her daily planner, and headed for the door. "Living with my father already did that."

# five

At eleven-thirty, Barley's favorite downtown café was already crowded, but Jake and Olivia found a booth at the back. That suited Jake, who had spent the last hour prowling the town while he reassessed the enigmatic, disturbing Olivia Sinclair.

She wasn't turning out to be a female version of her father. In fact, she reminded Jake more of a fragile, wild bird about to be shot down by a hunter. And Jake was the hunter.

They slid into the sagging vinyl booth. Jake eyed the soiled, mostly handwritten menus propped between the condiments. "You'll have to recommend something," he said. "It's been years since I was in a place like this."

"What *do* you do, Mr. Donovan, other than act as your sister's avenging angel?"

If her words had been sarcastic and challenging, Jake would have verbally carved her into pieces. But the question was voiced softly, with an undercurrent of restrained humor. Her demeanor—even when Jake continued to sit there without responding—remained one of self-effacement. Like she was some blasted whipping boy, waiting for him to wield the whip. Or a wounded bird poised for flight.

"I do anything I please," he bit out, more angrily than he intended, since this woman was destroying all his preconceptions of her, and making him feel about like the

Marquis de Sade in the process. Irritably plowing a hand through his hair, he growled an apology that stopped short of a totally honest explanation. "Sorry. I've never been fond of crowds."

Olivia glanced around, smiling a little. "If this bothers you, may I suggest you bypass the mall on Saturdays."

The overworked waitress came to take their order, her manner brisk but not unfriendly. She knew Olivia, and suggested the daily special. "It's extra-good today," she said.

They ordered two plates of cubed steak, mashed potatoes, and butter beans.

"At least you're not one of those vegetarian nuts who pretend a bowl of lettuce is the most fulfilling meal in the world," Jake commented.

"No, that's Maria. We argue about it all the time, but so far neither of us has convinced the other to recant." She studied him a second, looking indecisive. "Um . . . could you expand a little on your 'do-what-you-please' lifestyle?"

There was a moment of awkward silence. Olivia studied the table and Jake studied her, then shrugged, bowing to the inevitable. "I'm a sometime professional mountain guide, ex-pro football wide receiver, occasional adventure writer, and a few assorted other things I won't go into now," he reluctantly offered. He hated explaining himself, especially to this woman. But considering what he was fixing to propose, he figured he owed her at least that much.

"That explains it," Olivia said, surprising Jake even more. He had steeled himself for the usual feminine gushing or the equally feminine censorial commentary on his "selfish" lifestyle—not that short, cryptic response.

"Explains what?" he ended up having to ask when Olivia refused to elaborate.

Her sidelong glance brimmed with apology and wariness. "You seem . . . untamed, and very aware of your power. Last night—" She hesitated, then shrugged and admitted, "Last night you frankly scared me."

Jake leaned forward. "Well, Ms. Sinclair, you're frankly surprising *me*. And I don't like surprises."

"Why?"

Again, that disconcerting, almost ingenuous aura so contrary to what he'd expected. Jake found himself responding just as honestly. "In my experience, surprises can cost you your life." He sat up as the waitress returned with two steaming plates overflowing with the kind of hearty meal he'd forgotten existed on the planet.

And then—even as Jake looked on in consternation— Olivia bowed her head and closed her eyes.

"What are you doing?" he growled under his breath. "This is a restaurant, not a church, for crying out loud."

She ignored him, finished the brief silent prayer, and began to eat.

Jake followed suit, then laid down his fork. "You know, this is going to be incredibly difficult if we don't set things straight right up front."

Olivia put her fork down as well. "I agree." Leaning forward, she asked forthrightly, "Exactly what is it you're going to require of me, Mr. Donovan? I've already decided to go along with it, as long as it's not illegal or—" She colored slightly—"immoral."

"Call me Jake, and you forgot 'fattening.'" His mouth twitched at her look of incomprehension. " 'Illegal, immoral, or fattening,' " he quoted, smile broadening when she stared across at him as if he had two heads.

"You're teasing me," she accused incredulously.

"Yeah, Ms. Sinclair, I guess maybe I am." He toasted her with his iced tea. "So—now that you can see I'm not a rampaging madman, and I've discovered your eyes turn completely blue when *you're* teasing and rain-washed gray when you're nervous, I suppose we'd better hammer out the details of your . . . penance, did you call it?"

"Here?" She glanced around, still looking flustered.

"You don't seem to have a problem praying in public, so why worry about some old prunes overhearing the terms of your sentence, so to speak?"

"I hardly call blessing the food before I eat 'public praying.' As for—"

"Do you do that all the time?"

"Do what?"

She was really getting rattled now, Jake realized, a little taken aback by the spurt of intense satisfaction zinging through him. On the other hand, a disconcerted, uncertain Olivia was infinitely easier to manipulate than the controlled robot of last night.

"Pray," he said. "Do you do that a lot?"

"Um . . . before meals, yes. At night always. When I'm lonely, scared, don't know which way to go. Why, Mr. Donovan?"

"Jake."

Pressing her lips together, Olivia began folding her napkin, the movements crisp and deliberate. Jake watched, silently laughing, the savage need to humiliate changing rapidly to an exhilarating game of oneupsmanship. It was a game he thought he'd lost all interest in playing years ago.

The waitress paused at their table. "Everything all right here? Y'all want dessert?"

"It's delicious as usual, Maggie, but I'm afraid Mr. Donovan and I have to be going." Before Jake quite knew what she was about, Olivia had pulled out her wallet and handed some money to the waitress. "Thanks again. Keep the change, okay?"

"You're mighty welcome." She gathered the dirty dishes and left.

Without a word, Olivia rose and headed for the door.

Jake waited until they were out on the sidewalk. "Thanks for the lunch, Ms. Sinclair, but the—"

"Olivia," she interrupted, flicking him the small purring smile of a kitten who didn't know any better than to tease the tiger's tail. "If I call you Jake, you have to call me by my first name."

"Olivia," Jake growled, teeth clenched. "Don't patronize me again, lady, or you'll think my behavior last night was pretty tame." He held up a hand, cutting her off. "And lest you misundertand, I don't have a problem with a woman paying for my meal . . . unless she's paying for the sole purpose of scoring points."

Olivia turned pale and silent. They walked down the sidewalk, past her shop, to the parked rental car. He opened the door, but Olivia didn't get in.

"I'm sorry," she all but whispered. "You're right, I shouldn't have paid for your lunch without asking you first. I—I don't know what came over me." She cleared her throat, spoke a little more firmly, though she avoided meeting Jake's narrowed gaze. "I'd like to know what you have in mind, so I can tell Maria where I'll be and when I'll be back."

"What's the matter, Olivia? Don't you trust me?"

"No—o. But I called your sister this morning, and I'll just have to take her word that you're basically a decent man who'd never dream of hurting someone weaker and smaller. She did warn me that your temper's as hot as a jalapeño pepper, but no matter what my father did to her and Davy, you wouldn't harm me . . . uh . . . physically."

Jake eyed her with grudging respect. "I hope she also warned you that with Davy pretty much out of the picture, I'll do whatever I deem necessary to take care of my sister—" He paused, then added with a provocative grin— "legally, of course."

"Of course," Olivia echoed. "Well . . . she asked me to pass along a message to you whenever I thought the time was right." She halted.

The little minx was leaving him dangling again, just as she had in the café. Propping his elbow on the car door, Jake determined to wait until they rolled up Barley's sidewalks if necessary.

A cloud crossed over the sun, and Olivia tugged her raincoat close, looking cold but collected. "I've decided," she finally announced to the lamppost Jake had leaned on earlier, "that her message can wait a little longer."

*So . . . you do have a backbone,* Jake thought, finding that the realization pleased instead of angered him. Soon he'd find out whether that backbone was made of straw or steel.

"We're driving to the outskirts of Charlotte," he told her. "And today I'll have you back by five. Now, you've got two minutes to tell someone before I come to fetch you."

She was back well within the time limit and slid into the passenger seat with an uncertain smile.

Jake leaned over, close enough to cause her to press back against the seat. "Listen to me," he ordered, very quietly. "I've played a lot more vicious hardball than you—than your 'ax man' of a father, even. I know how to read people, know what they're thinking, what they're going to do even before they themselves know." He smiled coldly. "So if you choose to play games with me, Olivia Sinclair, be prepared to lose. Because believe me, you will."

Olivia gazed straight up into Jake's face with haunted eyes. "I know." She stopped, her throat working. "I know all about the games people play," she finished in the most poignant voice Jake had ever heard.

"I doubt it." He straightened and came around and slid in beside her. "I seriously doubt it, lady, but it doesn't matter, since the only game you'll need to be worrying about for a while is the game of survival."

He started the engine and backed out without another word.

## *six*

After driving forty-five minutes toward Charlotte, Jake turned off the freeway onto a winding state road. Sitting beside him, Olivia finally broke a long uncomfortable silence, torn between amusement and anxiety. "So . . . where *are* we going?"

Jake chuckled deep in his throat. "I wondered how long it would take." He glanced down at his watch. "Twenty-seven minutes. I have to admit that's the longest a woman has ever sat beside me with her mouth shut."

He was baiting her deliberately, of course, but Olivia learned fast. She wasn't going to touch *that* comment with a twenty-foot pole. "My father hated distractions when he drove, and idle chitchat headed his list of distractions." She didn't add that Jake's caustic tongue rivaled her father's. If she possessed any survival instincts at all, Olivia knew she should end this whole business right now, before Jake Donovan cut his way past all her defenses.

Before lunch—a lifetime ago—she'd promised Maria that Jake couldn't chew her up. Well, Olivia was wrong.

Glancing across at his hard, unforgiving profile, she had to repress a sudden shiver. Even if she were to insist, she had a feeling Jake wouldn't let her go now. He needed to see her pay for her father's misdeeds as much as Olivia needed to atone for them. There was no alternative. Whether she liked it or not, Jake Donovan was her ticket

44

to freedom, her best and final bargaining chip.

Nothing else over the past humiliating weeks had turned out as she'd planned. God had to have sent this man her way, and that meant Olivia had to endure whatever Jake dished out. *I'll do whatever I have to, Lord. I promise.*

They entered the outskirts of Charlotte, and now Jake turned into an almost deserted parking lot. Across the cracked, weed-infested pavement, Olivia spotted several ramshackle buildings, one of which looked like an old house. She bit her lip, anxiety intensifying when a filthy, ragged old man shuffled into view, ambling toward the door of one of the buildings.

"Yep," Jake answered the unspoken question, "we're here." He slid out and came around and opened Olivia's door. "Come on, Olivia Sinclair. It's time for you to see for yourself what happens to people who've been stripped of all their pride, their ability to produce. People who become nothing but helpless pawns in the hands of powerbrokers like your old man."

As if she didn't already know. Clutching her purse tightly, Olivia meekly followed Jake across the parking lot, down a sidewalk that turned into a muddy path, and through a door sadly in need of paint and new hardware.

"Yo, Sherm!" Jake called out. "We're here."

Olivia took inventory. The large room had once been some kind of warehouse, she guessed, now transformed into a shelter. Tables and chairs of every size and description riddled half the floor space, with another area for sleeping, where a dozen or so cots were neatly lined up. On closer inspection, she could see that several were occupied. Men, and a few women, of all ages—disheveled and beaten-down—sprawled in the chairs, on the floor, or wandered aimlessly about.

Smells assaulted Olivia's nose. Always sensitive to odor, the nauseating scents of unwashed bodies, musk, and mildew—and the repugnant aroma of steamed brussels sprouts—almost sent her scrambling back out the door. Then she caught Jake's eye.

Smug, malicious satisfaction swam in the arctic gray, and a frankly wicked grin twisted his mouth. Swallowing hard, Olivia turned her back, watching the approach of a huge potbellied man with a balding head and full salt-and-pepper beard. As he came up to her, Olivia noticed with a jolt that he also had a graying ponytail streaming halfway down his back.

"Hiya, J.D. Glad you made it," he rumbled in a gravelly baritone, extending a hand the size of a cast-iron skillet. "Put 'er here, my man. It's been a while since I've seen you—two years, you ornery cuss. Now introduce me to the little gal here who stirred up your carcass enough to drag me outta my bed two nights ago with some harebrained notion."

Jake shook hands, pummeled the man's back. "Olivia Sinclair, meet Sherman Piretti, owner, director, chief cook, and bottlewasher of Sherm's Shelter." He winked. "Sherm and I spent our pro football years with the same team. He was a 'Sherman tank' of a linebacker."

Speechless, Olivia felt her hand grasped and gently squeezed. "We just go by first names here," Sherm informed her, eyes twinkling. "And I'll tell you right now, 'Olivia' is too much of a mouthful for me. Whaddya think, J.D.? You've known her longer than I have. What do you call her?"

Jake's gaze moved over Olivia in a leisurely study.

"We-l-l," he drawled, "she doesn't really strike me as a 'Livvie' or even 'Liv'—" The wicked grin deepened.

Sherm eyed Olivia thoughtfully. "She's a little bit of a thing, J.D. You sure she's up to this? Most of these characters around here have seen more of the inside of a cell than they have a church."

Olivia decided enough was enough. "I can handle anything I have to," she announced. Hopefully the calm pronouncement disguised the quaking uncertainty weakening her knees. "And my name is Olivia. O-LIV-i-a."

Jake shook his head. "Stubborn, isn't she, even though she's the perfect candidate for martyrdom. But I trust you to take care of her for me."

The two men traded significant glances.

*Oh, boy,* Olivia thought, her own glance sliding over the motley assortment of pathetic souls scattered about the room.

"You know I'd walk on hot coals for you, J.D. 'Course you might not know most of these do-good church women give up after a trip or two out here."

Olivia stiffened in outrage that turned to astonishment at Jake's next words. "She won't give up," he promised. "She might break, Sherm, but I have a feeling she won't give up. And I'd better warn you—she's a born time manager, so be careful, or you'll find yourself as regimented as we used to be the week before the play-offs."

Sherm shuddered playfully, looking like a benign, balding Santa Claus. "Right. So . . . every other evening and one weekend a month, starting next week, right?" The two men shook hands, then Sherm was patting her shoulder. "Don't look so worried, O-LIV-ia. Who knows? Maybe you'll end up as this year's Mother Teresa—"

"You could have discussed the schedule with me, at least," Olivia observed on the way back to Barley. "I do have a career, you know, and other people are depending on me."

"You promised to do whatever I demanded, as long as it wasn't immoral or illegal. Since you set the terms yourself, I figured you'd already arranged all your fancy planner books accordingly."

Olivia sighed. There was no rebuttal to that. Leaning back, she closed her eyes, unable to shake the vivid memories, the appalling smell of Sherm's Shelter. *Lord, what have I done?*

She'd read the papers, seen the news, listened to her father gloat. She knew the homeless and disenfranchised were out there, knew their numbers were growing—some, yes, because of her father. The knowledge had tormented her for years, long before Jake Donovan  showed up.

Out of genuine concern—and guilt—she'd contributed love offerings through her church and prayed with the rest of the congregation. But until today it had never occurred to her to offer her services.

She'd built a demanding career, and her time—like Jake had pointed out so bitingly—was organized right down to the minute. *Months* of careful planning had been required to ensure that The Bridal Bower could operate without her supervision for just three weeks.

Yet she had promised Jake. More than that, she had promised herself . . . and she had promised the Lord. She had no choice but to follow through on Jake's plan. Of course, penance which ultimately led to absolution required great sacrifice. The last month had hammered home that bitter lesson.

Olivia prayed this time the payment would finally unlock the choking slave collar that had tormented her for so many years.

Night had fallen by the time Jake dropped her at The Bower to pick up her car. "Don't bother," he warned as Olivia automatically stepped toward the door of the shop. "We need to talk, so I'll follow you home. Whatever you planned to do here will have to wait a little longer."

*You brought this on yourself,* Olivia reminded her grumbling conscience as she turned onto her street some ten minutes later. Maria had warned her, Rollie had warned her . . . but then, Maria and Rollie hadn't spent the past almost twenty-seven years ashamed of their last names.

She turned into the driveway, and the headlights of her car flashed onto the house, illuminating the porch and windows. Olivia slammed on the brakes, gaping in horrified disbelief.

Streaks of scarlet paint and dozens of shattered eggs marred the entire front of her humble little cottage—smeared, oozing down the clapboard and windowpanes. Spatters and slimy drops clung to the bushes below the windows. The last of the bucket of paint had been poured over her welcome mat.

Olivia flung herself out of the car, dashing forward with an incoherent cry. She stopped short of the door, and stood frozen on the walk—stunned into immobility—wondering helplessly who could possibly hate her this much.

Unnoticed, Jake came up and took her arm. "Go back and sit in your car," he ordered, voice hard, commanding. "Whoever did this might be hiding somewhere close, waiting to see your reaction."

"My house—"

"I know. I'll help." Olivia stared up at him, uncomprehending. He sounded . . . concerned? "Come on, Olivia. Stay here in the car. Don't move. I'll be back in a minute."

Moving soundlessly, Jake slipped around the side of Olivia's house, alert for any movement or noise. The first rush of adrenalin had eased, but every nerve ending from the back of his neck to the tips of his fingers, prickled. He cursed silently, fluently. Obviously the little martyr had stirred up a hornet's nest with her idiotic plan to seek forgiveness in behalf of Sinclair. That was the only plausible explanation for the sickening mess out front— and the one he intended to bully Olivia into explaining to the police.

Nobody was hiding around the house.

Jake tested the back door, found it still locked. After making a complete circuit of the yard, he returned to Olivia's car, which was empty. Alarm poured over him in a scalding rush until he caught sight of her stooped figure, fumbling with a wad of useless tissues at the front porch. Stubborn, stupid woman! Jake stalked across the lawn, preparing to scorch her ears.

Then he heard the sound of soft, strangled sobs. Anger evaporated as a flood of compassion caught him totally off guard. Reaching down, he lifted her resisting body completely up and away from the disgusting mess.

"You have to leave it until the police have seen it," he reminded her gently, tugging out his own handkerchief.

"Maria warned me," she choked out, the words husky, her voice thick with tears. "She told me I shouldn't go around reminding people of what my father had done to

them. Rollie agreed. They both said I was asking for
trouble—"

Jake wiped her hands, listening, trying to ignore the
welling pity—and the fresh anger against the person or
persons who had hurt Olivia. He didn't want to deal with
those kinds of feelings, not now. Not with this woman.

"They were right." He gave up trying to clean her hands.
"Come on, we'll go through your back door. They apparently left everything else intact. You can clean up while I
call the police."

She jerked away. "I don't want to call the police. They'll
find out who my father was . . . I'll lose all my customers,
have to move to another town. I'll—I'll—"

"Stop it." He took hold of her upper arms and admin-
istered a light shake. The yellow glare of the front porch
light cruelly illuminated her wild eyes and tear-streaked
face. Beneath his hands her bones felt fragile as a bird's.
Slumped and helpless, Olivia looked utterly humiliated.
*That's what you wanted, pal, remember?*

"Come on, Olivia, get hold of yourself. Where's the
calm, controlled woman I first met? The one who stared
me straight in the eye and threatened to call the police?"

"I—you're right." From somewhere, Olivia dredged up
the will to pull herself together, and Jake watched the
return to sanity with reluctant respect. "I'll . . . just get my
purse." She stepped away, took a shuddering breath.

Inside, Jake made coffee while Olivia washed her hands
and face. Then he made her sit and sip while they waited
for the police. Because she was just staring into space like
a zombie, he found himself talking to her, chattering like
a blasted magpie to fill the aching silence. He couldn't
stand the uncomprehending pain darkening her eyes.

". . . and after I left the pro sports zoo, I was so sick of people and their power games, I spent two years prowling wildernesses all over the globe. Hey, did Beth tell you we grew up in the mountains west of here? Maybe that's why I love wild areas so much. Not so many people there trying to get in your face." He paused to check Olivia's color. "Drink all your coffee, that's it. I know, it's stronger than yours, so make all the nasty faces you like, but drink it down."

The Barley police arrived—a grizzled sergeant with a paternal streak and his younger sidekick. They took photographs, wrote down Jake's and Olivia's statements. The younger cop, a homely young man with milk-pitcher ears, spent a lot of time consoling Olivia, pointing out how sick some folks could be and how she shouldn't take it personally.

Olivia stared at him with her big eyes gray as a raincloud, and finally smiled a heartwrenching smile. "I *have* to take it personally," she said. "Whoever did this knows I'm a Sinclair."

The two policemen had never heard of Alton Sinclair, so Jake filled them in. When they were finished, he walked them to the back door, thanking them for coming, for promising to keep an eye on the area.

"You her boyfriend?" the young cop asked.

"I'm working on it," Jake responded, deadpan, then wondered why he had said that.

Revealing the present nature of their relationship would probably put his name at the top of their list of suspects. Besides, they'd never believe Olivia's warped sense of Christian ethics. Jake himself was having a hard enough time dealing with it, since he couldn't even remember the last time he'd set foot in a church.

When he returned to the living room, Olivia was reading through the daily planner she kept on the hall table. "It must be one of the people I went to see," she murmured, still looking like a gray-eyed ghost. "I suppose I should be grateful for *your* restraint, shouldn't I?"

Jake mentally replayed a few old calls from his football days until he had his temper under control. "Yes, you should," he agreed, voice deceptively mild. Reaching down, he cupped her chin in his hand, stroking the incredibly soft skin. "I told the police I was working my way around to being your 'boyfriend.' Be careful, or I just might be tempted to act the part."

# seven

Armed with ladders, old cloths, buckets, and the garden hose, Maria, Rollie, and Olivia canceled all appointments and spent the entire next day cleaning the front of Olivia's house. Fortunately the capricious February weather cooperated, providing a cool, clear morning and sun-warmed afternoon.

"I suppose I should be grateful they left the inside intact," Olivia observed at one point, glowering at the still pink porch. They'd tossed the welcome mat in the garbage. The police had confiscated the empty paint can.

"Are you sure you don't want to stay with me for a week or so?" Rollie asked. Again. Olivia had spent the previous night in the spare bedroom of her assistant's apartment. Roaring about in chenille bathrobe and fuzzy slippers, Rollie had berated Olivia, Jake, the vandals, and the dissolute condition of the entire world, punctuating each diatribe with offers for Olivia to move in with her for a while.

"You did tell Mr. Troublemaker Donovan you wouldn't be going to that—that place for the time being, didn't you?" Rollie asked now, plump face glistening with perspiration even though the temperature by late afternoon had dropped to the forties. "It's bad enough you're at the shop during the daytime, but leaving your house alone at night is asking for trouble." She wagged a red-tinged finger at Olivia, adding significantly, "And not just the house."

Olivia wrung out a rag and flopped back on one of the lawn chairs they'd dragged out front. "Rollie, you and Maria are worse than a baker's dozen of mothers."

"Speaking of mothers, have you told her yet? When does she come back from her cruise anyway?"

A dilapidated little car pulled into the driveway and stopped, sparing Olivia the necessity of a reply. The door opened, revealing a thin, youngish woman who hesitantly made her way up the path. Her face registered consternation and dawning dismay.

Olivia stood, walking slowly over to greet Beth Carmichael, Jake's sister.

"Oh, dear. Jake said it was bad, and I can see that it was, even though you've cleaned up a lot." She smiled at Olivia, the expression in her brown eyes so like Jake's that Olivia's heart jerked painfully. "I'm really sorry."

"Thanks. Um . . . what are you doing here?" Olivia waved a self-deprecatory hand. "I don't mean that the way it sounds—I'm just surprised." Maria came up beside them, her look questioning. "This is Maria Santinas, my friend and partner at The Bridal Bower. Beth Carmichael, Jake's sister."

Beth seemed awkward and nervous. "I wanted to talk to you, but this obviously isn't a good time." She shifted, tugging on a strand of straight brown hair hanging limply in unstyled layers about her care-worn face. "The trouble is, I've only got this afternoon . . . I have to be at work by six."

Maria glanced from Beth to Olivia. "Take her inside and we'll pack it up out here. It's getting too cold and dark to work anyway," she said, overriding Olivia's protests.

Faced with both hers and Rollie's mule-headed insistence and Beth's fidgeting, Olivia led the way inside.

"I'm sorry," Beth apologized again, sitting down on the edge of the chair and looking even more uncomfortable.

"Don't be ridiculous." Olivia collapsed onto the couch and heaved a sigh. "Actually, I'm beat, so you gave me a wonderful excuse to leave the pair of them to clean up. Now they can complain about me to their hearts' content."

Beth relaxed, finally. "Well . . . in that case . . . I wanted to talk to you about Jake. About what he's trying to do to you."

Massaging the back of her neck, Olivia sent Beth a dry look. "He doesn't have to try. He can intimidate and scare the heebie-jeebies out of me with a single look."

Beth leaned forward. "He hasn't a clue you feel that way, Olivia. I knew I needed to come talk to you. Jake's never behaved like this before—rock-dumb about a woman, I mean. You don't need to be intimidated by him. The only reason I haven't interfered before now was because Jake promised me you were doing this because you wanted to, not because he forced you."

"Do you do that a lot? Interfere in your brother's life?"

Beth looked appalled. "Goodness, no! Nobody tells Jake what to do. Probably the last person who tried is six feet under." She clapped her hand over her mouth, looking, if possible, even more horrified. "I didn't mean . . . he would never—"

"Don't worry. I know you're joking." This time Olivia was careful to let Beth know she was serious; Jake's sister needed reassurance.

Once again the memory of Olivia's behavior the previous night intruded. She'd been so shocked by the assault on her house she'd actually lost control and cried all over Jake like the worst sort of hysterical female. The kind her father had belittled the most. Alton Sinclair had known how to turn on his infamous charm, coaxing the victims to bare their souls, encouraging them to sign anything he put in front of them. Then he'd reduced them to tears—and laughed in their faces.

But Jake hadn't laughed at all. Olivia also remembered—vividly—the feel of warm, incredibly gentle fingers stroking her chin. Jake possessed mind-melting charm as well, but it wasn't anything like her father's.

Olivia straightened her shoulders. "Beth, I don't pretend to understand your brother, but trust me, I'm not naïve or stupid. I spent a lifetime living in the same house with a man who derived great pleasure from making people squirm, watching their pain—" She broke off abruptly, staring straight up at the ceiling until an unexpected rush of tears subsided. "I do know Jake isn't like that. The trouble is, I don't think he can understand that I'm not like that either."

Beth shook her head violently. "He does know. It's just that for so many years he—we've both hated your father—" She shrugged helplessly— "which unfortunately translates to all things Sinclair—"

"That's why I'm willing to do anything to get people to forgive him," Olivia pointed out, weariness dragging at her words.

"Olivia—" Beth's face scrunched up. She pondered her wringing hands a minute, muttering half beneath her breath, "I have to do this. He's acting so strange, and I just know—" Her voice trailed away. She looked up, apparently determined to say what she had on her mind. "Jake's always gone his own way, but he's also always protected me, ever since I can remember. Our parents died when I was three, you see. My aunt and uncle raised us, mostly my aunt. She wasn't . . . very nice."

"I don't think—" Olivia began, uneasy with such stark revelations.

But Beth shook her head again. "Hear me out. I've thought about this for days, and I think you should know that I admire what you're trying to do, even though I disagree. I also love my brother, and you need to understand where he's coming from, so you don't—won't compare him to your father."

Olivia smiled a bittersweet smile. "Jake might share some similar traits here and there, but I'm convinced the resemblance is strictly superficial. I know inside he's nothing like my father." *God help me, please don't let him be like my father. . . .*

Beth looked brighter, but far from convinced. "Oh. Well, anyway, I want you to understand him. Maybe it's because I was younger, such a wimp. I was always shy, not real assertive, you see. Jake took care of me, protected me. A kid at school stole my lunch once, when I was in fourth grade. Jake got hold of the bully and dragged him two miles—all uphill—to our house, forced him to apologize. And Jake was only twelve himself. He's been that way about me all our lives, like I told you. But what you may not realize is that he's like that with anyone—anything—weaker and smaller and helpless."

*I don't want to hear this*, Olivia thought. Her defenses against Jake, flimsy from the beginning, were in danger of crumbling with every passionate word pouring out of Beth's mouth.

"That's why he was almost ready to kill your father after what happened with me and Davy. Why, when he found out about you, he hot-footed it back here and hunted you down, breathing fire. Then . . . when he realized what you're really like—" She glanced at Olivia, hesitating, looking irresolute.

"You might as well finish it," Olivia prompted. "Go ahead, I can handle it. What does Jake really think of me?"

Hot color seeped under Beth's skin. "I know. I'm an interfering busybody."

"But you love your brother. I wasn't making fun of you, Beth. Maria, the girl you met outside, keeps reminding me how nobody knows when I'm teasing or serious. Well— I was teasing you, okay?"

Beth nodded, looking relieved. "Okay. Jake did mention how your eyes turn blue when you're teasing, and I can see they are, except now they're turning darker because of what I just blabbed, right?"

The anniversary clock on the end table chimed the half hour, and Beth's hands flew to her cheeks. "Oh, my! I have to hurry. Olivia, no matter how aggressive Jake might come across, he'd cut off his hand before he'd really hurt someone. That's one of the reasons he quit playing football. But he's also as stubborn as the granite in Grandfather Mountain, and he isn't going to drop this ridiculous notion to teach you a lesson." She stood. "That's why you have to convince him to drop it. Your father's dead and gone, Olivia, so why don't you get on with your life instead of—of trying to make up for what he did to Davy and me?"

"Do you go ever go to church?"

Nonplussed, Beth shook her head. "No, except maybe

at Christmas, every so often. I took Davy last year, but he started crying so we left early. Why? What on earth does church have to do with all this?"

Olivia winced.  "I learned something at church once that really struck me hard, as the daughter of Alton Sinclair—" She paused. "There's this verse in the Bible that warns us about the sins of the fathers and how they'll be passed on to their children. Well, it's true. All my life I've been an outsider and a scapegoat—a pariah. Nobody wanted to be my friend. And in high school, the guys rarely asked me for dates, no matter how nice I tried to be. I don't know why I always took it more personally than my brother and sister. Mom says it's because I'm the youngest, and my father got worse in the last ten years of his life—"

She rose, running her hand over tense neck muscles. "Anyway, I can't live like this anymore. That's what I tried to explain to you when I visited you that day. The Bible also talks a lot about paying for our sins, about how the Israelites had to make all these sacrifices. Well, I'm going to pay for what my father did—as much as possible, that is. That's why I don't care what your brother has in mind, as long as we work around my business commitments."

"Olivia, you don't know—" Beth began urgently.

But Olivia shook her head. "I do know. I'm insane, crazy, stupid, and stubborn like your brother." Olivia angrily swiped at a tear. "But I'm also desperate. I want to walk down the street and not be afraid of people. I want to live where I don't have to worry about coming home to—" She waved her arm toward the front window—"to this. Why do you think I invest every penny I make in my business, instead of my home? I want to sleep at night and feel good about who I am. And if dishing up nauseating food to dirty, downtrodden bums a few months results in Jake—and you—forgiving my father, I'll do it. Then I'll be free."

Beth searched Olivia's face. Suddenly she reached out a reddened, chapped hand and took hold of Olivia's clenched fist. "Somehow, I think it's you who need to forgive your father. Not Jake. Or me. Or anybody else you may have approached. Maybe if you can just let the past go, you'd be able to sleep at night, instead of torturing yourself. Or letting my brother manipulate you like you were one of the radio-controlled planes he used to play with."

"Model planes?" Olivia grabbed a tissue from a box beside the anniversary clock. She mopped up, feeling ashamed and ridiculous. And thoroughly defensive. *She* needed to forgive her father?

"You know, those remote control toy planes people fly? They do all sorts of loops and dives and crazy stunts, and the person on the ground just stands there and enjoys the process, risk-free."

"I—see." Olivia managed a watery smile. "Well, I suppose I'd rather be a toy airplane than a puppet."

Beth giggled. "Okay. I quit. Besides, I have to go."

They walked through the kitchen to the back door before Beth spoke again, humor gone, the urgency back in her voice. "Olivia, the other reason—the main reason—I had to come see you was to because Jake wants more from you than a couple of nights a week at Sherm's Shelter. Even though I talked with him until my voice was hoarse, he won't back down. Olivia, he's going to make you visit

Davy at the sanitarium, spend a day there every weekend.
And that's too much to ask, no matter whose daughter you
are."

# eight

Wet and rank from two days without a bath, muscles pleasantly aching, Jake rappelled down the last twenty feet of rock to a ledge eight feet above the ground. In a burst of joy over his unfettered freedom, he unclipped the lines, then free-jumped the remaining feet. Stupid, of course, and as unprofessional as a tenderfoot, especially on a slushy February day when the winter earth was still hard and unforgiving.

Right now Jake didn't care. For the past week he'd mother-henned an endless succession of clumsy, jabbering parties on half-day hikes around the winter wonderland of the Shenandoah Mountains in Virginia. As a free-lance guide for Adventures Unlimited, he normally enjoyed the chance to introduce novices to the wilderness. This time, after sending off the last group, he'd disappeared up Hawksbill Mountain, trying to recover his inner balance. Trying—also unsuccessfully—to wipe all thoughts of Olivia Sinclair out of his mind.

No matter whether he was sweating up the park's highest peak, or stretched out in his sleeping bag, Olivia's face intruded. And in his ear, Beth's voice called him every name from "stubborn goat" to "the reincarnation of Alton Sinclair!"

That last accusation was the one Jake couldn't shake. He'd thoroughly lost it with Beth, stormed out of her apartment ten days ago and hadn't returned. Yeah, okay.

He'd behaved like a boor—the quintessential surly male. Now, freed from his climbing equipment, Jake flopped down with his back against a boulder, and proceeded—once again—to justify his actions.

First and foremost, independently of any pressure from Jake, Olivia had virtually given him carte blanche to "work out her penance."

Second, Beth had initiated everything in the first place by requesting his help, hauling him home from the best vacation he'd enjoyed in years. She had no call to criticize his game plan.

Finally, his idea for Olivia to help at Sherm's Shelter had been designed to benefit both parties—a lesson for Olivia and assistance for Sherm. What was so evil and manipulative about that?

Jake tossed back a slug of water from his water bottle, then dug out a pack of M&Ms. Munching thoughtfully, he recalled his last conversation with Sherm. His old football buddy had warned him that Olivia was acting like a cross between an unseasoned rookie and the coach.

"She works hard, never complains. But she's been sick in the john twice . . . though she don't know I know. She's also taken a couple of the regulars under her wing, so to speak. Trying to reason with them." Sherm laughed. "She just don't understand the mentality, J.D., old buddy. Seems to think the only thing most of these bums need is encouragement and a chance, and they'll be transformed into pillars of society. A few of them do just need a helping hand, but most have chosen to drop out permanently. I tried to warn her, but you're mighty right about her take-charge mentality."

Shaking his head, Jake had to grin. That was Olivia, all

right.

But Sherm's final words gave Jake a headache. "She's got this book-thing in her purse, sweet-talked real names out of half a dozen of our folks, and wrote every blasted one down in that book. Promised she'd try to help. Last night she spent more time trying to instill the Puritan work ethic than she did dishing out vegetable soup."

Recalling the conversation now, Jake pinched the bridge of his nose, knowing he was going to have to straighten out Ms. Sinclair himself. She was supposed to weep over the condition of those poor slobs, not wade in and draft improvements.

As soon as Jake returned, he'd be taking her for her first visit with Davy. Trying to make sense out of his pathetic, drooling brother-in-law would teach her a needed lesson. *Yeah, that would bring her to her knees, but good. So why don't you feel vindicated, Donovan?*

Breathing deep soothing lungfuls of tangy mountain air, Jake finally conceded what had probably been inevitable almost from the very beginning, when he'd watched Olivia defending her shop. She'd stood there so poised and professional, calmly threatening to call the police because she actually believed Jake might start trashing the place. And she hadn't backed down an inch, even though Jake could snap her in two with one wrist.

Then—less than twenty-four hours later—he'd seen Olivia with all the barriers down, shell-shocked and bewildered as a child, tears streaming down her face while she tried to comprehend the ugliness of hate-fed violence. That this Olivia was so diametrically opposite the Olivia in her store was a paradox that left him feeling sandbagged. Sandbagged—yet exultant.

He wanted her, on all levels.

For the first time in over a decade—maybe his entire life—Jake was consumed with need for a woman that surpassed the physical. Persistent, inevitable as the tides, the depth of his feelings washed over him, sweeping him to an inescapable conclusion. He wanted Olivia Sinclair, all right . . . but he also wanted to protect her, understand her, shield her from the slimeballs who'd vandalized the front of her house.

Above all, he wanted to force from her mind forever all thoughts of atoning for her rattlesnake-mean father, so she would see Jake as a man—not just the means to an end. She couldn't erase the past, and she'd certainly never be able to whitewash Alton Sinclair. Why couldn't the woman just accept that fact, for crying out loud? But no, not Olivia. Nope, Ms. Sinclair had to trail around the countryside, babbling religious tripe about "earning God's forgiveness in her father's behalf."

All she'd earned so far had been a far more human form of vengeance, first from Jake . . . and now from some lunatic fruitcake.

"What kind of God shackles His people like that?" Jake found himself asking aloud. "She's nothing but a walking, talking bundle of shame and guilt. I don't need a God like that—and neither do you, Olivia Sinclair." Starting now, he determined to persuade her to break out of all those religious chains, and focus on more important things— like Jake.

Decision made, he popped the last piece of candy in his mouth and rose, eager to fetch Olivia. Moving automatically, he broke camp, his mind sifting through possibilities, probabilities—and certainties. The lady didn't know it yet, but she was his.

Singing golden oldies at the top of his lungs along with the car stereo, Jake headed down the mountain, toward Barley.

Unfortunately, Olivia had already left for the shelter, a distinctly unfriendly Maria informed him just before closing time the next afternoon.

"I hope you're satisfied with yourself," she berated Jake, gesturing with a handful of silk flowers. "Olivia's always been quiet, reserved . . . but she used to laugh, too. Now she looks like a scarecrow, and all she talks about is how she's 'earning forgiveness' by helping those pathetic people at the shelter. She has a wedding next weekend . . . and I actually had to remind her of the date. She's never been absentminded like that."

Jake casually snagged the silk flowers out of Maria's hand and dropped them on a nearby table. "You look like an expensive vase," he observed, mouth twitching when Maria appeared ready to ignite into flames. "In the first place, Olivia agreed to the arrangements, as I'm sure she told you. In the second—not that it's any of your business—it's her father who's to blame for any and all of her compulsions. Not me."

Plonking her hands on her hips and tossing her curling black mane of hair, Ms. Santinas thrust her face right up next to Jake's and hissed, "You better not hurt her, Jake Donovan! She's too good for the likes of you, and don't you think I don't know it. Why I let you charm me into telling you where she lived—" She stopped abruptly. Her jaw sagged. "Her house—"

"Don't even think it," Jake snarled. "I was with her that

night, you recall. And no, I didn't 'arrange' for someone
to do it for me. If I were you, Ms. Santinas, I'd be trying
to convince Olivia to watch her back, her house, and this
place a little more closely for a while. The police can't
monitor the place twenty-four hours a day, and unless I'm
mistaken, whosever trip wire Olivia stumbled over is just
warming up."

Olivia's assistant stared round-eyed at Jake, momen-
tarily silenced. He plucked one silk rose from the table and
headed for the door. "Have a good one," he tossed over his
shoulder.

An hour later, he surveyed the large room where he'd
brought Olivia two weeks earlier, noting the changes.
Curtains adorned the windows. Bouquets of artificial
flowers, like the rose he was holding, were artlessly
arranged in empty bottles and jars. A makeshift bookcase
had been constructed out of boards and concrete blocks
and now sported a ragged collection of used books.   All
Olivia's doing, Sherm had informed Jake when he arrived.
Apparently she brought something every time she came.
Right now she was outside, in the back.

"Some old geezer showed up the other day with an
injured Canadian goose in tow," Sherm related. "Threatened all manner of bodily harm to me and anyone else who
called the humane society, or tried to hurt the bird." He
tugged his beard, looking disgusted.

"So what's that got to do with Olivia? And why did you
let her go outside—alone in the dark, for Pete's sake—
with an unknown transient?"

Sherm wiped his hands on his apron, favoring Jake with
the kind of knowing look that always made him very

uneasy. "Well . . . it appears your little bird's charmed the socks off that old man, and the two of 'em treat that goose like it lays golden eggs. Never saw the like. And if you think I have any better luck than you telling that gal what to do, you're a whole lot dumber than you used to be. J.D., old buddy, my instinct's fairly screaming 'bout this one. Best get out while you can."

He left to return to the kitchen, and Jake leaned on the doorjamb, wondering if he should confront Olivia now, or wait until she came inside. When she still hadn't appeared in three minutes, he tossed the rose on a folding chair and headed out the end door.

Moving quietly, he maneuvered his way along a muddy path, easily visible even in the dark because of the security lights Sherm had installed the previous year. At the corner of the building he stopped, peered around the corner—and froze.

Sitting cross-legged in the dirt with the goose in her lap, Olivia was quietly stroking the graceful bird, one of whose wings inclined at an ominous angle. Across from her sprawled a little old man. In the bright artificial light, the three figures presented a surrealistic, almost macabre tableau. Especially since—on top of layers of shabby rags—the wheezing old boozer wore a lovely, and very feminine, lavender knit sweater.

Incensed both by Olivia's careless generosity and her reckless disregard for potential danger, Jake stalked across the yard. The goose sensed his presence first and started to struggle. Olivia turned her head, eyes widening even as she soothed the agitated bird. "Jake! You startled us." Firmly but gently she secured the bird's head. "Shh—it's okay. He won't hurt you."

"Just let him try," rasped the little old man, who staggered to his feet, weaving slightly. One hand searched beneath the layers of clothing.

Jake tensed, readying his body. "Hello, Olivia. Nice goose," he offered, not taking his gaze from the old man.

"You can't have my bird!" The old man took a step toward Olivia. "This goose is mine!"

"Don't worry, Eddie. Jake's a—a friend. He won't hurt your beautiful goose any more than I will. Did you know he's climbed mountains all over the world? He loves wildlife, too—"

"Olivia," Jake interrupted, keeping his voice low with an effort, "I think maybe you'd better give Eddie his goose, and we'll go inside."

She started to say something, met his gaze, and closed her mouth. Eddie had finally succeeded in pulling a knife free, and now he brandished it at Jake with menacing intent.

Consternation flitted across Olivia's face. "Eddie, you know the rules," she remonstrated before Jake had a chance to speak. "If Sherm catches sight of that, you'll have to leave. He might even call the police."

"Olivia—"

"You stay outta her face, man!" He took a wavering step toward Jake, who feinted easily aside.

Olivia surged to her feet, goose and all. "Eddie, stop! You shouldn't do that." The goose began wildly flapping, honking, and Olivia was forced to let the creature go free. Unable to fly, it beat a noisy, awkward retreat toward the darkest corner of the lot.

"Now look what you've gone and done!" the old man yelled, words ending in a squeak as Jake's hand clamped

down on his wrist and twisted. The knife dropped. Jake
shoved the man aside and retrieved the weapon, straightening to face two pairs of accusing eyes.

"For crying out loud!" he snapped at Olivia. "I didn't
hurt him."

The old man didn't say anything for a second. He just
stood, looking shriveled and old and defeated. Behind
Jake echoed the wrenching honks of the frightened goose.
Abruptly, the old man turned and ran, disappearing into
the darkness.

"Eddie, wait!" Olivia started after him, but Jake grabbed
her arm.

"No—you'd only humiliate him more."

"But he's leaving his goose." She pulled away, straining
to see around him. "Jake, we have to find him . . . we have
to help the goose."

"Okay. Quiet, honey. . . . We'll find the bird. I love
wildlife, too, remember?"

She quit struggling, her expression almost stunned.

Jake sighed, mentally kicking himself. "Don't look at
me like that," he muttered. "Come on, let's go find the
bird. She can't be too far."

"How do you know it's a 'she?' " Olivia asked, totally
irrelevantly, Jake thought.

"I don't. But the squawking and flapping are definitely
female."

Olivia wisely resisted a retort, and they crept together
toward the sound of the goose's diminishing cries. "Over
there," Olivia whispered. "By the fence, in those weeds.
Jake . . . she's frightened. Please be careful."

In the darkness, Jake could barely make out Olivia's
silhouette, but he didn't need to see her to know that the

huge eyes would be smoke-gray with pleading. Did she really think he was such a monster? "Try to talk to her, distract her, and I'll sneak up on the other side—"

An hour later an amazingly tame Gretel (so dubbed by Olivia) was nesting comfortably at the back of a small enclosed pantry. Olivia hand-fed the bird, crooning nonsensical phrases as if it were a baby and insisting that Gretel would be much happier inside.

Sherm called a woman licensed to rehabilitate wild game who promised to come for Gretel as soon as possible. In the interim, the goose could stay here where she'd be safe, warm, and well fed.

Olivia orchestrated the whole procedure with heartfelt earnestness and such unarguable logic that everyone ended up falling beneath her spell as tamely as the goose. With every third breath, she also counseled Sherm to take pains not to let anyone hurt or frighten Eddie's bird.

"I think she's pretty much yours now," Sherm pronounced, scratching his beard thoughtfully, "though I can't promise she won't turn into somebody's supper before that wildlife gal comes to fetch her."

Roaring with laughter, he watched Jake trying to convince an irate Olivia all the way out the door that Sherm had been only joking.

Jake had almost succeeded in reassuring Olivia that Gretel was safe from harm when they reached the parking lot—to find all four of Olivia's tires slashed.

## nine

The senseless destruction hit Olivia in the face like a bucket of raw sewage. "I don't believe this," she whispered, shivering in the dampening night air. She walked around the car twice, Jake, seething with rage beside her.

"Jake, could you control yourself?" she eventually suggested in a normal voice, so calmly Jake broke off midsentence to peer down into her face.

"Olivia? Are you all right?"

This time she'd show him she wasn't such a blithering idiot. "Of course." She cleared her throat, offering brightly, "Though I don't mind confessing to a certain queasiness. I've had to be cautious all my life, you see, since I'm Alton Sinclair's daughter. But I never—" Her voice trailed away as they moved into a patch of light and she glimpsed Jake's face. The intent, predatory expression would have terrified her two weeks earlier, but Olivia knew better now.

She wondered—hating herself—if he would comfort her with the same tenderness he'd shown the other time, when she had cried like a baby. *Olivia, your brain has turned to mush.*

"We'd better alert the police to put out an APB on your friend Eddie," Jake announced. "And after we call, I think I'll rip a strip off Sherm's hide for letting you out of his sight in the first place. When I think of you, outside in the dark alone with a knife-wielding derelict—"

"I don't think it was Eddie," Olivia returned, hugging herself, trying not to think about her favorite lavender sweater or the grain of truth in Jake's analysis. "He's not that kind of person."

"And just how do you know that?" Jake demanded. "There's no telling how many other assorted weapons he might have hidden under his clothes."

She didn't want to dwell on that possibility. Exhaustion sucked her toward a dark pit full of questions which Olivia wasn't prepared to handle right now. "He wouldn't," she repeated, struggling to summon words to make Jake understand. "I've gotten to know him. He . . . trusts me because I like Gretel, because I was nice to him."

Jake snorted. "Sweetheart, you need a crash course in reality. You think just because you're 'nice,' these poor slobs won't take advantage any way they can? They're desperate and devoid of self-esteem, remember." He growled something beneath his breath. "I must have been out of my mind to start this. Look—your car's a textbook example. We're dealing with the dregs of humanity here—society's victims. The 'have-nots.' Most of them aren't overly fond of the 'haves'—especially guys like your father."

"You're forgetting something," Olivia pointed out, leaning wearily against the side of the car. "Eddie wouldn't have known which car was mine." She lifted her chin. "It wasn't Eddie."

A light bulb clicked on in her brain then, triggering chills that feathered down her spine as Olivia faced a far more alarming possibility.

Jake started to say something, but checked himself. He stepped closer, staring down at Olivia. "Hey," he finally murmured, and it was the melted-chocolate voice he'd used once before. "C'mere." He gently tugged her into his arms, holding her head against his shoulder. "It'll be all right, Olivia. I promise. Trust me."

Trust the man whose uppermost goal was to humiliate her, make her crawl? Yet Olivia's hands crept up and burrowed into the folds of Jake's leather jacket. She was cold and shaken. And now she was also afraid. "Jake," she whispered, feeling the steady, reassuring beat of his heart beneath her ear. "Jake, what if it's the same person who threw the eggs and paint against my house?"

Ensconced in Sherm's private quarters, which turned out to be the small house Olivia had wondered about the first time she'd come here, they met with two patrolmen assigned to the case.

Nobody listened to Olivia's protests, not after Jake gave the officers Eddie's knife and recounted what happened out in the yard. Or rather, nobody listened until Olivia—equilibrium partially restored after choking down half a mug of Sherm's bitter coffee—calmly insisted on the possible connection to the vandalization of her house.

"My father was Alton Sinclair," she finished, watching as awareness dawned on one of the policemen. Her father's reputation unfortunately had spread as far as Charlotte.

"I remember . . . he died back in January, didn't he? Sorry, ma'am, though from the little I heard, he wasn't likely to be mourned too much." He cleared his throat, shifting uncomfortably.

"It's okay." Olivia dredged up a smile. "But I think we have to face the possibility that some recent actions I've taken might have incurred the—the vengeance of one of my father's many victims."

"That tears it," Jake muttered.

Olivia fumbled in her purse for the daily calendar. Explaining her visits to various people over the last month—and her motivation—she carefully withdrew the list of names and handed it to the now riveted policemen. "I'm not trying to cause any trouble, or make any accusations," she promised, praying she was doing the right thing. "But if there's a chance someone is—" She stiffened her shoulders, stood straight—"is taking out their anger on me because my father's dead and beyond reach, you need to know the circumstances."

"Yes, ma'am. We'll contact the county boys as well as—" he checked his notes—"Sergeant MacClary in Barley. In the meantime, ma'am, may I suggest you keep your eyes open. And limit the time you're alone."

Jake drove her home, face grim, manner forbidding, almost as if he were angry with her. He didn't say much, stuffing Olivia into his leather jacket, fastening her seat belt himself, then punching in a cassette of sixties oldies.

*So much for my foolish dreams of a little tenderness and a few gentle words from Jake,* Olivia scolded herself. If she weren't so distracted and admittedly unnerved, she would have pursued the matter. Instead, she tried to focus on the music instead of Jake's stone-wall silence, and the policeman's parting words: *This might turn out to be a stalker. Been a rash of them the last couple of years. You be careful now, Ms. Sinclair.*

Unfortunately, unless the stalker was caught committing a crime, there was little the police could do.

"Olivia."

She turned her head, unconsciously inhaling the comforting smell of leather and Jake's clean, uniquely masculine scent. "Yes?"

"Have you ever been . . . involved . . . with anyone?"

*Why on earth would Jake want to know?* "What exactly do you mean by 'involved?'" Olivia countered, suddenly uneasy.

"You're not married, or even seriously dating, from what I can tell. And over these last weeks, there's been no mention of a man in your life. Seems a little strange, considering your vocation."

Well, at least he was finally talking, and he didn't sound cold or sarcastic. Probably he was just trying to divert her, keep her from dwelling on what had happened. "No, there's nobody like that in my life. Never has been, to be honest." She shrugged. "A lot of it's probably my fault. By the time I was old enough to date, I already carried enough shame to sink an ocean liner." There's 'sin' in 'Sinclair,' she recalled bitterly "Besides, who'd want to risk messing around with Alton Sinclair's daughter?"

She was glad it was dark so Jake couldn't see her face. Huddling deeper in his jacket, Olivia marveled at her flapping tongue. "My junior year in high school, there was this new boy. He didn't know about my father, and we used to talk, eat lunch together. It was wonderful. Then a group of kids decided to enlighten him about the 'Typhoid Mary' he was hanging around with. The next day at school when he tried to avoid me, I figured out real quick what had happened."

"And then?" Jake prompted.

Olivia shook her head. Here she was, spilling long-buried hurts to the man determined to crush her spirit. She must be an idiot, a masochist.

Then she smiled a twisted smile. Who was she fooling? Neither Jake's motives nor her own crusade mattered. She didn't understand how it had happened, but she wanted— needed—Jake to treat her as if she were a person of worth. Talk to her in that deep smooth voice of his, soothing raw spots on her soul that she hadn't realized until now were still hurting. Okay, so what if she was behaving more like a starry-eyed high-schooler rather than a grown woman almost twenty-seven years old? Right now she was too tired to care.

"I assured him my father only hired hit men to rough up guys over the age of eighteen. Then I turned my back and walked away before he could walk away from me. And I promised myself that someday I'd persuade everyone that my father wasn't really that bad."

"Except he was," Jake growled, half under his breath. His hand reached out and ejected the tape. Silence filled the car.

Olivia's tired mind focused abruptly, leaving her un-sure, on edge. She wondered if Jake's conversational forays were deliberate instead of random, since he be-haved more like a man pursuing a goal than a man trying to soothe a beleaguered woman. His next statement confirmed her uneasy suspicions.

"Why don't you just change your name legally, go by your mother's maiden name or something? Disown your father and the past like the rest of your family did and get on with your life?"

The words mimicked Beth's almost exactly. They must have decided to join forces. "I can't. You know that."

Without warning Jake pulled the car over and stopped,

turning toward Olivia. "You know what? You're twisting me into knots. Nothing I've planned concerning you has turned out like I intended. Nothing." He shook his head. "When Beth called me last month, all I could think about was how I planned to inflict maximum pain and humiliation upon the person I figured had to be a carbon copy of Alton Sinclair."

"The realization hasn't escaped me—" Olivia muttered, feeling the intensity of Jake's emotion battering her with increasing force. Straining to see his face in the dark interior, all she could make out was a brief, unpleasant smile.

"Yeah . . . then I finally met you, and ran smack into your corkscrewed Christian notion of crawling around prostrating yourself on behalf of a man who patently doesn't deserve it. Between that—and some kook out for revenge—I don't know whether I'm calling the shots here or ducking out of their way." His fingers drummed an angry tattoo on the steering wheel. "I used to wonder about religious people, with their interfering noses and sour expressions, spouting off do's and don'ts and acting miserable. After meeting you, I don't wonder why anymore."

Lifting his arms behind his head, Jake stretched, rotating his neck and shrugging—a lean, formidable man who played to win. Who used words like weapons when he was thwarted. He'd even warned her.

Hot and cold prickles raced over Olivia's skin, leaving her slightly nauseated. "I'm not like that," she denied, but her words—unlike Jake's—lacked conviction.

Suddenly his arm dropped down on the seat behind Olivia, his fingers tucking her hair behind her ear, then tracing a path around its contours and down her jaw. "I thought a lot about you the last couple of weeks, up in the mountains. About what kind of God you feel compelled to placate in such a degrading manner. And you know what I concluded?"

Mute, Olivia shook her head, feeling the brush of his fingers against her neck before he finally moved his hand away. "I'm glad I don't have to deal with your God," Jake purred. "Sounds to me like He and your father would have made a great team."

Olivia flinched. "That's not true! You don't understand. My father was cruel and sadistic . . . he—he manipulated people. That's not what God does. Jake, listen to me. I'm trying to make everything right—like Jesus did when He was willing to die in our place. If I can pay for some of what my father did, then I won't feel this horrible, unbearable shame anymore. I won't have to hide out in a town where nobody knows the name of Sinclair. I'll be free." Faint tremors rippled through her body as she willed Jake with all her might to understand. "That's why I know God sent you to me. I believe you're His instrument. Helping at the shelter, visiting your brother-in-law . . . I'll do it all! I'll do anything, like I told you. And then—" Her voice caught—"then I'll be free."

"So. Now I'm elevated to the status of God's emissary instead of a hair shirt," Jake intoned, the low vibrations lifting the hairs on Olivia's scalp. He shifted again, moving closer, forcing her back against the car door. "And you'll do anything I want—"

Olivia's heart slammed against her rib cage. She couldn't take a breath. "Um . . . I'm not sure—"

Now his fingers pressed against her lips, stilling her

words. His head was suddenly a hair's breadth away. "Well, guess what, my little martyr. I happen to want you. Like I said, nothing has been going the way I planned thus far. But since you've just promised you'll do anything I want, maybe this is the time to mention it—"

Olivia went rigid. She was trapped, helpless, and all by her own hand. Once, Jake had tenderly held and comforted her. More often he'd goaded, mocked her. But until now she had never really been afraid of him. All the warnings, all the precautions over the years had flown out the window because she'd refused to heed the signals. Now she'd played right into Jake Donovan's hands, and there wasn't a thing she could do about it.

In a whisper of movement, he was kissing her, a kiss that promised to grow more demanding. Olivia froze, still as a cornered mouse. Keeping her lips tightly pressed together, squeezing her eyes shut, she withdrew deep into herself and waited for the onslaught, like she used to do when Daddy was in one of his gloating moods. She was stupid. Stupid, naïve, and foolish. Beth had been all wrong about her brother. Rollie and Maria had been right, and now Olivia would pay the price for her inexcusable blindness.

"Olivia, open your eyes. Honey, open your eyes. I promise I'm not going to hurt you."

He was stroking her arms gently. The voice—the one like warm melted chocolate—poured over her spirit. "Shh . . . it's all right. Don't pull away from me, okay? I'm not going to hurt you, Olivia."

She opened her eyes and gazed unblinkingly up into his face, wondering how he could look so hard, so unnervingly savage, yet talk to her so gently. "Are you finished?" she asked, distantly ashamed of the weakness in her voice.

"Boy, lady, you just scared me—" He paused, and took a deep breath, his expression softening. "Thank God. You're back with me."

Olivia realized all of a sudden that he was still holding her, his hands moving slowly from shoulders to wrists, warming her, calming her. And it was working. She felt her muscles unclenching, one by one, though a querulous voice inside denounced her continued weakness and stupidity. "I didn't think you believed in God."

"Right now I'll take all the help I can get," Jake returned. He studied her for a moment. "I'm sorry. I had no idea. I was angry and frustrated and—and, I'll admit, aroused, but I never meant to scare you like that. Never in my life have I hurt a woman, no matter how flaming mad." A corner of his mouth lifted. "But then, I've never met anyone quite like you either. I'll try harder in the future to avoid lambasting you full force." He finished and said, very gently, "Okay, now?"

Somewhat to her surprise, Olivia nodded. "I guess so. Beth was right. You do have some kind of a temper. But you didn't . . . insist . . . uh, you didn't force—" She floundered, relief and shame causing her to stutter. "It was one of those games you told me you play all the time, right? And I—I messed everything up?"

His hands slid down to cover hers, rubbing his thumbs over the backs. Olivia tried to ignore the strange warmth creeping up her veins, melting the ice and causing shivers of an entirely different kind.

"Olivia Sinclair," Jake eventually murmured, dropping a feathery kiss on each palm, "I don't know what I'm going to do with you. And since nothing has been working like

I planned . . . I have a feeling it's going to be totally different from what either of us expected."

# ten

The next day Jake called the editor of an outdoor magazine. The guy had been bugging him for months. By the following night, he was on his way to the southern Chilcotin Mountains in British Columbia to research a horsepacking photo safari outfit.

"What changed your mind?" the editor wanted to know. "When we talked last, you told me you'd be unavailable until May at the earliest."

"My plans changed," Jake snapped. "Fax me the info at this number." He read it out. "I'm booked on a flight to Seattle Friday."

Over the next days—most of which were spent snowbound in the main lodge—Jake nonetheless learned a good bit about Big Game Trails. He definitely approved of the outfit's commitment to shooting big game with cameras instead of guns. Garrick, his host, a wiry former rodeo rider from Wyoming who played a mean harmonica, placed safety for the client at the head of his list. And while not cordon bleu, the hearty meals available would satisfy most appetites. The magazine article Jake had agreed to write would be a definite thumbs-up.

He also learned one other inescapable fact: Olivia Sinclair was driving him nuts.

"I don't think she's an iceberg, exactly," Jake shared with Garrick late one night. "I just don't think she knows how she feels."

The two men had spent all day tromping through the snow, following tracks and having a whale of a time. Buoyed by the easy camaraderie that had sprung up between them, Jake had relinquished most of his usual tight-lipped reticence. Beyond that, Garrick projected a rare inner peace that invited a very confused Jake into his confidence.

"A couple of times I caught her watching me with this yearning expression on her face," he continued. "I'm familiar enough with that kind of look, I suppose, to recognize what it means." He acknowledged Garrick's snort by toasting him with his mug. "Except Olivia added a dimension I haven't confronted. She sends out the kind of nonverbals that tell me she wants me even if she wouldn't quite know what to do if she got me. Then, when she did, she was terrified out of her skull—" Jake paused. "My mood wasn't the best, of course. I had all these grand plans how I was going to initiate certain . . . changes . . . in our relationship, only Olivia snarled the lines—first with her naïve faith in the inherent goodness of all humankind, then with this blasted stalker business. I'll admit my timing was lousy, but I never expected her to freak out."

Garrick roused himself from his favorite spot by the fire to throw on another log. The rest of the staff had long since gone to bed. He and Jake might have been the only two men alive for a thousand miles. "Got no use for teasing women," Garrick drawled. "Baiting you with come-on eyes and smiles, then trotting out a saddlebag full of no's just to watch a man squirm."

"Olivia's not like that," Jake mused. Reeling with exhaustion, some subliminal portion of his mind cringed at this whole conversation. "I told you about her father?"

"The four-flushing three-piece-suit slimeball?" Garrick chuckled. "Yeah, you told me. No wonder she's messed up four ways to Sunday. Beats me why you don't dump her, 'specially after what happened in your car that last night."

A battering wind whistled down the mountains behind Garrick's timberframe lodge, rattling windows. In the fireplace, a burning log crumbled, sending a shower of sparks up the chimney. Sitting across from Garrick in a comfortably deep chair, hands wrapped around the mug of hot apple cider, Jake should have been contented. Instead, he was restless, uneasy as a mustang at mating time.

"She probably thinks I've dumped her," he finally admitted, staring into the flames. "But I had to get out of there. I told you how it all started—how I'd planned this perfect revenge for what happened to my sister and her husband—" Suddenly his line of reasoning took an unexpected turn. "Garrick, tell me . . . you ever think about God?"

Garrick scratched the plaid flannel shirt over his stomach, and pondered the ceiling. "Well, I guess you might say the two of us share more than a nodding acquaintance. Sort of hard up here, y'see, not to accept the existence of Someone more powerful—and a whole lot smarter—than us poor mucked-up humans." His gaze dropped back to Jake. "You've been all over the world, man. I've read most of the articles you've written over the years. How can you see what you've seen, do the things you've done, and not think about God?"

Jake sipped cider and watched the fire. "Don't know," he eventually offered. "My sister and I lost our folks when

I was nine and Beth was six. My mother's older sister raised us. She was a hardbitten mountain woman, and my uncle spent most of the time staying on the job to avoid her. He worked for the forestry service. The only time I remember hearing God mentioned was when Aunt Sophy threatened us with His wrath when we acted up."

Garrick grunted. "Know what you mean. Met a few religious harpies like that myself."

"The years I played pro football," Jake went on, "there were a few guys who called themselves born-again Christians. They used to spout off high-sounding phrases about Jesus, especially when we won. But most of them didn't act much different from the rest of us, and I more or less ignored what they said.

"And when I'm climbing a mountain, or kayaking down a river, I just enjoy the incredible freedom. No ties. Nobody telling me what to do and how to do it. Wondering what's around the bend, on the other side—"

"You're still missing something, Jake. I can hear it in your voice, and don't try to tell me I'm wrong. Sometimes a man lays down tracks as easy to read as a herd of big horns, for anybody smart enough to read 'em." Garrick pondered the ceiling some more. "It's not just that messed-up woman you're pining for as hard as you're running from." He left off studying the exposed timber beams and scooped up his harmonica. "Might be you're missing out on getting to know God. Think about it, fella." He put the harmonica to his lips and closed his eyes, ending the conversation.

Much later, Jake lay in bed listening to the wind, while Garrick's words played over in his mind like the haunting melodies of his harmonica. On many levels Garrick reminded Jake a lot of himself—confident, assured of who he was, living the life he'd chosen to the fullest. But Garrick wasn't uneasy and restless, like Jake.

If Garrick did have some sort of "relationship" with God, it was a lot more comfortable one than the relationship Olivia struggled with every day. Her perception of God reminded Jake uncomfortably of the wrathful, punishment-minded Being Aunt Sophy used to threaten would fill Jake's britches with fire and brimstone if he didn't straighten out.

Jake hadn't wanted anything to do with that kind of God then, and—like he'd told Olivia—he didn't want anything to do with Him now. There was no freedom in living out a life full of fear, waiting for God to strike if you so much as made one wrong move.

If Jake ever decided to look into the matter, he'd go for Garrick's God, no doubt about it.

As for Olivia, well, Jake had chewed that one over more than he cared to admit for almost two months now, but he couldn't wriggle out of a couple of certainties. First and foremost, he'd blown it royally with the woman, treating her like he had, then running like a scalded cat. He owed her an apology.

The other certainty made him squirm even more uncomfortably: he was still attracted to Olivia Sinclair more than any other woman he'd ever known.

Yep, he'd learned a lot up here in the wilds of Canada, and that last lesson was by far the scariest.


On a warm and sunny March day, Jake returned to North Carolina. For the first time in his life he paid scant attention to the frothy pink and white dogwoods, the hot pink azaleas, and butter yellow forsythias splashing the surroundings in joyous bursts of color.

Dumping his gear on Beth's threadbare but immaculate living room rug, he hurriedly showered and changed, intent on making it to Olivia's shop before closing time. Fortunately Beth was at work and couldn't yell at him about the mess.

On the way to The Bridal Bower, Jake decided it was time to buy himself a car, instead of paying the usual outrageous rental fees he put out every time he stayed with his sister. Money was no problem; he had money to burn in investments, mutual funds, and banks all over the world. That in itself was a joke, though Beth's categorical refusal to accept more than token financial aid never ceased to rankle. Money had never been one of life's consuming passions for Jake, even though fate had capriciously blessed him with some semblance of a Midas touch. That is, he didn't care as long as he had enough to support his nomadic lifestyle.

Of course, buying his first car in eight years confirmed the radical shift in a few of those priorities. If he bought himself wheels, would a regular job with regular hours follow? A house with a white picket fence and a couple of dogs on the doorstep, for crying out loud?

Turning onto Main Street, Jake fought another terrific inner battle not to pull up at the nearest pay phone. In two hours or less he could be on a plane, headed anywhere he pleased—if he chose to keep running.

Olivia's storefront loomed through the windshield. The Bridal Bower. If that name didn't send a man high-tailing it out of town, he had to be as crazy as Davy, his poor slob of a brother-in-law. Davy had checked out of reality because he hadn't been able to cope with failure, or with all his responsibilities.

The skin at the back of Jake's neck crawled, big-time, but he didn't look for a pay phone.

He lifted his foot off the accelerator just as a couple emerged through the store entrance. Faces glowing, they were talking with Olivia, and Jake couldn't tear his eyes away from her graceful elegance, even dressed as she was in a simple short-sleeved blouse and tailored slacks.

Several more young women spilled in a noisy, laughing tide past Olivia, who was holding the door while she talked. Jake couldn't hear the words but, knowing Olivia, it was probably a litany of last-minute advice to somebody's bridesmaids.

He drove on past and turned down the alley behind the row of shops, parking next to the vehicles he recognized as those belonging to Olivia's two assistants. There was no sign of Olivia's car.

He slipped in the staff entrance without a qualm, startling a plump older woman into dropping the phone. Jake picked it up and handed it back. "Don't mind me," he reassured her with a grin. "I'm just here to see your boss."

The woman slammed the receiver back into the cradle. "I don't think so!" she pronounced in ringing tones, rising to block the door into the main part of the boutique with her considerable bulk. "You're Jake Donovan, aren't you?"

"Pleased to meet you." Jake waited, hands casually stuffed in the waistband of his jeans in a seemingly nonthreatening stance. He wondered how Olivia's self-appointed bodyguard would react if he picked her up and dumped her back in the chair. She might weigh close to two hundred pounds, but he could manage it. On the other hand—

"You might as well let me through." He spoke congenially, confidentially. "It's nice that she has such caring friends, even when they are way off base."

Ms. Amazon folded her hefty arms across her chest. "You're butter-melting mouth and wolfish charms don't faze me, Mr. Donovan. Do you have any notion what Olivia's been through since you skedaddled to parts unknown?"

"No. What?"

The woman swelled as if preparing for battle. "She let you chew her up and spit her out like a piece of bad meat, regardless of what we tried to tell her. Even when you left, proving you obviously couldn't care less, Olivia still goes to that shelter every other night. Or at least she did until night before last, when she came out from church and found all the windows in her car smashed." She nodded once, double chins quivering. "Mighty suspicious how you were conveniently gone, if you ask me."

The good-natured teasing pose vanished. Jake took a step forward, tightly throttling back on his temper. *Be cool now, Donovan.* "What's been done?"

Lips pursed in satisfaction, her censorious glare reminded him uncomfortably of Aunt Sophy. But her next accusation almost sent him through the roof in spite of his determination not to lose his temper. "I'm surprised the police haven't already taken you into custody."

"Rollie, the Edgerton gang left so we can finally close up shop," called a familiar voice from an inner office.

"Did Maria remind you that they want us to go ahead with the reservations at—" Entering the room, Olivia caught sight of Jake and stopped dead. "Jake," she said, voice breathless, wary.

"Can we go somewhere and talk, or are the police already on the way?" *Not good, fella. You're supposed to keep a lid on it, remember?*

Olivia blinked, obviously recognizing the raw anger seething in the words. But she didn't retreat. Instead she whirled to face Rollie, who was hovering near Jake as if preparing to either tackle him, or dive under the desk out of harm's way. "What have you been saying to him, Rollie? You told him about the car, didn't you? What else? Davy? Even when you promised you wouldn't?"

Jake felt as if his rope had broken, dropping him into a bottomless void. "Davy? What are you talking about?" Ignoring an abruptly silent Rollie, he stepped right up to Olivia, muscles aching with the need to take her in his arms. "She told me about your car. She more or less accused me of untold crimes. But nobody mentioned Davy."

Olivia dropped her gaze, but Jake had seen the flare of alarm. "Olivia?" he repeated, softly, dangerously. For two weeks all he'd thought about was how he planned to make up, soften her with apologies and explanations so that, when he took her in his arms again, she'd welcome his kisses.

Once again, their reunion wasn't turning out like he'd planned.

"Rollie's overreacting," Olivia finally confessed. Drawing on that deep reservoir of control Jake admired, once again she managed to pull herself together. She glanced toward the older woman with a cool gray gaze promising retribution, then back to Jake. He wanted to kiss her, badly. "The police verified—through Beth—your whereabouts at the time of this last incident. I vouched for your presence the other two times and assured them I was solely responsible for triggering the stalker's actions. You're neither under suspicion nor in danger of arrest. Rollie, don't you have some phone calls to make? You can use the phone at the front register. While you do that, Maria can clean up out front."

"Olivia, I never meant—he deserved—"

"I appreciate your efforts, but I need to talk to Jake. Alone."

Grumbling but vanquished, Rollie gathered up a notebook bulging with protruding papers and left. Olivia gently closed the door behind her. Silence, throbbing and intense, filled the room.

"I'm glad you're back, Jake," she finally said, once again avoiding his gaze, "even though this is incredibly awkward. It would help tremendously if you'd quit glowering at me. We both know losing your temper's only going to make things worse."

Was his little manager taking him to task? Very carefully, Jake snagged a nearby stool, dragged it over, and lowered himself to the seat. His gaze never left Olivia. She was thinner, and purple circles marred the delicate skin beneath her eyes. But the steel spine was firmly in place, and though she was blushing now, she finally met his frank perusal without wavering.

Incredibly, Jake felt his anger subsiding. "All right," he promised amicably, hitching one foot on the second rung and propping his elbow on his knee. "The tiger's back in the cage. Satisfied?"

A corner of her mouth lifted. "How long will the tiger stay there?"

"Frankly, I'm not too sure. Probably not very long . . . if I don't get some answers." His voice hardened. "Tell me about Davy."

Olivia laced her fingers together. "I've spent the day with him the last two Sundays." The pulse hammered away in her throat. "I know that's where you'd planned to take me, before you left. Beth told me. She didn't want me to go, either, if it's any consolation, but gave in when I told her I'd go with or without her."

"A martyr mentality with a management obsession," Jake observed. "Deadly combination." He toyed with the stitching on his hiking boot. "So . . . what did you think?"

"I don't know how Beth stands it," she confessed. Moving restlessly, she wandered over to a counter behind Jake. "There's something else I need to say, something far more difficult than going to see Davy."

"Yeah? What could be worse than that?" He quit fiddling with his shoe and studied the graceful curve of her back, even though it was as stiff as a new pair of boots.

"I wanted to apologize for my behavior the last time we were together. I hadn't realized, until then, that I might have some major problems to work through on a number of levels."

He stood, hardly able to believe his ears. Olivia, apologizing to him? "Wait a minute. Back up. I shouldn't have come on to you when you were already upset over your car. It wasn't your fault. I was the one who was way out of line."

She still wouldn't turn around, seemingly wasn't paying

any attention. "I told you I hadn't really dated a lot, and the relationships I have been involved in never went much beyond the surface—" There was a tense pause. "That's why it never occurred to me that my father's destructive personality might have bled over into my ability to—to—well, that's my problem."

"Olivia—"

"—and you need to understand that I don't expect you to change your behavior just because I have a few problems," she rushed on. "It's just that I didn't think you really meant what you said . . . about wanting me, I mean, and—"

"Olivia . . . turn around and look at me." The words might have been harsh, but he made his voice sound as if he were crooning a lullaby. When Olivia whirled around, Jake crooked a beckoning finger. "Good," he smiled, a slow beguiling smile that usually performed magical tricks on feminine willpower. "Now . . . come here."

## eleven

Even though Olivia knew Jake was charming her deliberately, she responded anyway. She knew that Jake knew that she knew what he was doing, and her mouth itched with the need to grin a just-as-teasing response.

Only she was also afraid and unsure.

For weeks her emotions had swung wildly, from humiliation to anger to hope and then to despair. Because whatever either of them felt for each other, Jake wasn't a Christian.

Olivia had learned, both from her parents' experience and through her vocation, that unequal yoking almost always gives birth to unhappiness. *Lord, he's not one of Yours. I know that. Help me. I have to stop this. Now.*

"I don't know what will happen if you try to kiss me again," she confessed to Jake instead, and wondered if she had finally lost control of all her faculties.

Jake's smile deepened. "Neither do I," he returned. "That's why—since you have the protection of two spear-hurling Amazons in the next room—we're going to conduct a little experiment—" The slashing eyebrow arched—"with your permission, of course."

"Of course," Olivia echoed, as if that's what she had in mind all the time. She stopped three feet away—mouth dry, palms damp, knowing she should run, yet wishing with every rebellious ounce of blood in her body that Jake would just hurry up and do it.

"Give me your hands."

"My . . . hands? Why?"

Jake chuckled. "I'll show you." He held his out, palms up, but made no move to force her compliance.

Olivia stared first at the hands, then up into his face. All her breath escaped in a whoosh. "They're—they're damp. I'm sorry," Olivia stammered, lifting her hands and lightly resting them in Jake's.

"That's because you're nervous," he explained kindly. His fingers closed around hers, and he lifted them to his mouth. Kissing her fingertips, he captured her wrist, counting the pulse. He laughed softly. "You're not the only one. Maybe it's time you learned a few things about me—" Quickly he placed her hand over his heart—" before we *both* suffer cardiac arrest."

Olivia's jaw dropped. Beneath her hand his heart pounded in a hard drumroll as runaway as her own. She darted a quick look at him. "I'm not sure . . . you'll laugh at me—"

"Never. I'd never treat you like that. Look at me." His voice was so urgent Olivia obeyed instantly, meeting head-on his compelling, mesmerizing gaze. "I know I've bullied you, frightened you, treated you rotten, Olivia. And we both know about my lousy temper. But I promise you, I'll never ridicule you or put you down. We'll disagree—a lot!—and I'll probably continue to lose my temper every now and then, but I won't be trying to destroy your spirit, Olivia, ever again. You're one classy lady, even when you're fighting battles you can't win."

Gathering her close, he searched her face, the blazing desire softening into tenderness. "So . . . kiss me, sweetheart . . . please." His knuckles gently grazed her cheek. "And trust me. We can work it out, I promise."

They were standing so close Olivia could count the pulse beating strongly in Jake's throat, the same pounding rhythm as his heart. His warmth and strength enveloped her, but this time—instead of panic—she felt only a growing need to show him how she felt.

Tension pulsed between them. Resting both hands on his chest, her eyes drowning in his, Olivia leaned forward, lifting her face to his. She waited, but the horrible suffocating panic she dreaded still hadn't returned.

Dizzy, trembling with excitement and relief, she touched her lips to Jake's . . . and behind her the door flew open.

"We couldn't hear anything and Rollie was about to . . . oops!" Maria's voice intruded like a passel of uninvited relatives. "Sorry and all that, but . . . Olivia, are you sure you know what you're doing?"

Jake gently shifted Olivia to the side. "The door's behind you. Use it," he ordered in a pleasant voice that belied the look on his face. "If Olivia needs your help or advice, she'll call."

"That might be sort of hard for her to do the way things seem to be headed," Maria shot back tartly, unfazed.

Olivia squelched her roaring embarrassment and turned to face her colleague. "I'm fine, Maria. Truly. And I'll continue to stay that way if you leave us alone until I find out for sure—" She bit her lip, rattled and frustrated.

Maria's head tilted, though she did edge backward. "Find out what for sure?"

"Find out if I can kiss her 'til her toes curl," Jake supplied, smiling a knife-edged smile. "Scram, Ms. Santinas. Three's a crowd and all that."

"All right, already. I'm going! But I have a nice pair of

very sharp scissors and a special length of florist's wire set aside just for you, Jake Donovan . . . if you catch my drift?" She pulled the door shut, then reopened it and poked her head back through. "We have to be at First Street Methodist tomorrow at ten, remember." Accompanied by a healthy bang, this time the door stayed shut.

"Like I said, Amazons," Jake murmured. He shook his head, stretched, then cast a rueful smile toward Olivia. "Care to take up where you left off, or did friend Maria effectively douse all the flames?"

Olivia shook her head, then nodded, relieved by his easy acceptance of the situation. An upsurge of shyness choked her, but didn't constrain the seed of elation springing forth. "I didn't freeze," she said, and smiled. "I didn't panic at all!"

"Just the opposite, I'd say." Jake tapped the end of her nose. "Next time, Ms. Sinclair, I'll put out the 'Do Not Disturb' sign."

"Does this mean you're not going to escape back into the wilds of Canada, or someplace equally as remote, Mr. Donovan?"

A muscle twitched in his cheek. Then the corner of his mouth curled, and all of a sudden—to Olivia's surprise— he laughed. "It's a temptation," Jake admitted. "Except now that I've had a nibble or two, I'm afraid I won't be satisfied until I've made the catch." His finger followed the contour of her cheek, stopping to tilt her chin upward. "Tomorrow, Main Street Methodist at ten, right? See you then, sweetheart."

And he was gone.

That night Olivia called her mother. "I need to talk. Do

you have a few moments?"

"Of course, honey. I was just sitting here in the den, watching TV and relaxing." Abruptly her voice sharpened with anxiety. "Has something else happened? To you? The shop?"

"No—no. Everything's fine on that front. Or at least, nothing new since my car windows were smashed." Stinging nettles of guilt pricked Olivia's conscience. Her mother had returned from the month-long sabbatical cheerful and more peaceful than Olivia could ever remember.

Then Olivia had had to confess how her attempts to clear Daddy's name had resulted in the unpleasant attentions of "a probable stalker," as the police termed it. Now every time Olivia talked to her mother, she could hear a painfully familiar thread of anxiety weaving through all her words. Mama could understand neither Olivia's motivation nor her stubborn refusal to at least move in with Rollie. From then on, Olivia had carefully edited the events of the past two months, including Jake.

Unfortunately, now she was drowning—and her mother unknowingly held the only life ring that might allow Olivia to stay afloat. Taking a deep breath, she plunged in. "Mama, I've met this man, and—and I think I've fallen in love with him. Only . . . he's not a Christian and I'm petrified he might turn out to be like Daddy. So I—I have to know what Daddy was like when you first met him." She stared at her inexpensive framed print of Monet's "Wild Poppies" on the wall opposite the bed, where she lay propped against the headboard.

Until this afternoon Olivia hadn't verbalized the issue, hadn't even wanted to face it. She wasn't the most obedient Christian in the world, but she really did try hard to do the right thing, live a life that would be pleasing to God. She thought again of the Bible admonition about unequal yoking. Well, falling in love with an untamed, risk-loving, non-Christian adventurer was about as unequally yoked as two people could get! Still, she couldn't take the words back now, nor could she deny their truth any longer.

"Heavens, child, what a thing to spring on me at half past nine o'clock at night! Olivia, I don't know what to say—"

Olivia closed her eyes, picturing her mother—her thin hair prematurely gray from constant stress, the permanent wrinkle between hazel eyes which were always veiled, always uncertain. Her mother never looked at anybody directly, not even her children. Was that what Olivia would become if she committed her life to Jake Donovan?

"Mama, I'm sorry. I didn't want to upset you, but I need to know." Adopting the same calm, persuasive voice she used with recalcitrant clients, Olivia set about soothing her mother, gently coaxing her back to a calmer state, injecting humor at the end. "don't worry. I'm still you're cautious, controlled, fanatically organized daughter who's always on top of things."

Weak laughter floated over the line. "I declare, sometimes I wonder if your grandpa took a notion to inhabit your body. When you talk like that, you sound just like he used to, pulling our legs so sober and serious like, with a twinkle way in the back of his eye. Yours do the same thing, you know."

"So I'm told," Olivia agreed. Memories wrapped around her heart. "Mama, tell me about Daddy. Please."

The silence lasted so long she feared her mother would refuse, after all, even though Olivia had just bared her soul more openly than she had since she was thirteen years old. She clenched the receiver tightly, praying hard. *I have to know, Lord. Please, I have to know. Let her tell me, help me—*

"Your father," Mama spoke slowly, reluctantly, "possessed the looks and charm of Lucifer. And like the devil, he showed a body only what he knew they wanted to see. I was young. Headstrong, too, and a little wild, so it was so easy for your father. Olivia, honey, if this man is anything like that, you'd better run as hard as you can in the other direction."

Olivia kept her voice steady with an effort. "Did you have any idea, any clue at all what kind of person Daddy was before you married him?"

Another long moment of silence passed. Then, "Yes," her mother whispered, her voice shamed, full of sorrow. "And to my dying day, I'll have to live with the awful weight of it."

Olivia sat up, hardly breathing. "How did you know, Mama? What did he do?"

"He was subtle, oh, so subtle—and the time or two I actually questioned him, he always managed to talk me 'round . . . he was a master at twisting words even then." The voice grew hoarse, the words even more halting. "You remember that he never lost his temper? I used to think that made him so strong, so mature when, if I'd listened to my conscience, I would have known it was because he—he just didn't care. But at the time, I didn't want to see all the warning signs—"

"What signs?" Olivia nudged, holding her breath. "What

signs, Mama?"

Her mother's voice dropped once more to a near whisper. "His eyes were always . . . empty, if you really looked right at him. Empty behind the charm, I mean. And he—he teased animals. Nothing outrageously cruel, just tormenting. Making my pet dog beg for a treat, then throwing it in the trash instead of giving it to him . . . that kind of thing. And once—" This time the pause was so prolonged that Olivia was sure her mother had changed her mind about telling her story—"once we were out driving around . . . and a squirrel darted out into the road. Olivia, your father swerved . . . not to avoid hitting the poor little thing . . . but so he could deliberately *run over it.*" She finished on a whimper. "I'm sorry, baby, but it's true!"

"Oh, Mama—"

"He tried to brush it aside, convince me he'd never hurt anything so small and helpless, but I knew." Tears thickened the soft drawling syllables at last. "Deep inside, Olivia, I knew what kind of man your father was. But I told myself he'd change after marriage—I'd *make* him change. Just like you, baby. Just like you . . . trying so hard to see something good in your father. The difference is, I finally accepted the truth—"

There was another long pause. Olivia didn't know whether her mother was still there, or if she'd put down the receiver, too overcome with emotion to go on. Finally she spoke, her voice whispery-thin. "Olivia, if the man you're talking about is anything like that, I beg you . . . run away, honey. Run away before it's too late for you, too."

# twelve

Saturday morning. Judy Wells's and Barry Seymour's wedding. Part of The Bower's service for this particular couple included Olivia's presence at the church in her directorial capacity—professional but warm, authoritative but not dictatorial. Everyone and everything were depending on Olivia's seasoned, skillful handling to orchestrate a joyous, unforgettable day.

A little past six-thirty, just after dawn, Olivia rolled out of bed. Staggering like one of Sherm's drunken derelicts—and looking the part—she showered, dragged on a windsuit, then sat at the kitchen table and stared at a congealing bowl of cold cereal.

Perhaps a walk would clear her head. Rollie wasn't picking her up until nine-thirty. Olivia could make it all the way to the mall and back in that time. Maybe exercise and fresh air would accomplish what a sleepless night had failed to achieve—finding the words, the strength to tell Jake goodbye.

Letting herself out the back door and carefully locking it with the new deadbolt recommended by Sergeant MacClary, Olivia paused to inhale the fragrant aroma of dew on the honeysuckles and morning glories, and absorb the opalescent peace of early morning. With a sweeping scan, she also quickly confirmed that the stalker wasn't lurking about in the bushes between her cottage and the neighbors' houses.

An hour later Olivia trudged wearily back down the sidewalk, two blocks from the cottage. No words illuminated her soul, but at least a strange resignation had settled in her mind, allowing her to focus on the day's events instead of her own personal Gethsemane. She would somehow convince Jake that she couldn't see him anymore—but not because of any superficial resemblance to her father. How had her mother survived at all?

Over the years Olivia had attained a fair amount of insight into people and had dealt with every emotion from euphoric adoration to irrational temper tantrums. She was good with people . . . and she was cautious. After hearing about her father, Olivia was convinced Jake no more resembled Alton Sinclair than an ice cube resembled a glacier, except for one inescapable fact—neither man wanted anything to do with a personal God. Daddy had paid lip service on Sunday mornings to polish his image. A more honest Jake denounced religion openly—and so Olivia had to end it.

She might love him, be convinced he'd never hurt or abuse her, but Jake was not a Christian man. *I don't know why You're doing this to me, Lord, but I could really use Your help—*

Turning the corner onto her block, she waved to Mr. Potts, out watering his flowers. Birds darted about, chirping in the early morning sunlight. At least, it was going to be another beautiful day, perfect for a wedding.

Olivia turned into her driveway, idly noting the sputtering engine of an approaching car. She half-turned, catching the blurred glimpse of a small blue Toyota . . . and something hard slammed into the side of her head.

The searing pain exploded in her skull. A dark roaring

tunnel sucked at her consciousness while swirling lights blinded her. Staggering, fighting waves of nausea, Olivia tried to catch a last glimpse of the car. It was gone, the street empty except for the birds. She was too far away to summon Mr. Potts. She could never make him hear her.

*Got to make it to the house, Lord. I have to make it to the house . . . phone—*

Endless minutes later, her foot scraped the first step of the stoop at the back. She'd kept her wits about her long enough to make it to the back door, easier to unlock than the double set of locks on the front door. The swirling lights intensified. Then, mercifully, she blacked out.

Jake knew it was too early, but he also knew that if he didn't convince Olivia to leave with him before Maria or Rollie arrived to pick her up, he'd be up to his ears in antagonism. Flexing his hands on the steering wheel, he wondered why now—when his entire life had turned upside down—every female with whom he came in contact seemed bent on either ripping a strip off him or delivering a sermon.

The previous night, after blistering his ears over his slovenliness, Beth had delivered what could only be termed a harangue on his disgraceful lack of consideration for the feelings of others. Grimacing at the memory, Jake turned down Olivia's street.

When Beth put her mind to it, she could carve up a hog with her tongue. The grimace transformed to an anticipatory grin. Olivia, no doubt, would have something equally as astringent to say when he arrived without warning on her doorstep, practically at the crack of dawn.

He parked in the driveway, thinking as he loped up the walk that maybe after finishing up at the church, the two of them could spend the rest of the day in Charlotte, looking for a new car for him.

When she didn't respond either to repeated ringing of the doorbell or his pounding fist, a very unpleasant sensation slithered down his backbone. Senses heightened and alert, Jake checked out the front windows, all of which were completely covered by drawn shades. He sprinted around back.

Olivia was leaning against the door, eyes closed as if she were enjoying the morning sunshine.

Jake reached her in four long angry strides. "Didn't you hear the doorbell—" He caught sight of an ugly swelling bruise covering her right forehead all the way down to her cheek. "Olivia, what happened to you!"

Her eyes fluttered open and focused vaguely. Jake started to swear, caught himself, and clamped his teeth together while he dropped to his knees beside her.

Years of on-site first aid training took over. Running his hands over her limbs, he noted the rapid pulse, clammy skin, and shallow respiration. Early shock, perhaps . . . but at least there were no broken bones, no sign of blood, and she didn't seem to be injured anywhere except her head. He glanced around, searching for clues to what might have happened.

"Hello—" His gaze whipped back to her face. Vague recognition flickered in the blue-gray eyes. "I needed to be rescued by you . . . but then . . . I need to be rescued *from* you—" She began to slump sideways.

Jake caught her arm, shifted her body so he was sitting beside her on the stoop. Carefully he slid her into a protective embrace. "Olivia," he repeated her name gently, though his insides felt like an erupting volcano. "Can you talk to me?"

"I thought I was." Her voice was blurred, so laced with droll humor Jake wanted to shake her—or lay his head against hers and cry. What was the matter with him? And what did she mean, she "needed to be rescued from him?"

"Can you tell me now what happened to you? Did you fall, hit your head?"

Groggily she made an effort to sit up, slapping at Jake's restraining hands. "I'm fine. You don't have to hold me . . . and I have to be at the church—" She started struggling in earnest. "Have to get dressed. Have to be ready . . . let me go."

"Not on your life." Jake stood, swinging Olivia up into his arms, easily ignoring her feeble struggles. "Easy, honey. We need to get you to a doctor before we engage in a wrestling match. Shh, now—it's okay. We can still make it to the church in plenty of time."

She calmed, rested the uninjured side of her head against Jake's shoulder, a boneless, weightless bundle. A quivering sigh shuddered through the delicate frame. Jake remembered that weeks earlier he'd compared her to a wild and fragile bird. Wincing, he closed his mind to the poignant memory and started walking.

"I never realized . . . how strong you were."

He slanted her an incredulous look, using every ounce of his massive willpower to keep her from seeing he was scared right out of his own thick skull. "It has its uses. You're strong too, sweetheart, where it really counts."

Her eyes drifted closed, and a tear trickled down her cheek. "No, I'm not. I'm trying, I really am. But I'm not strong."

They reached the car. Carefully he lifted her in, then cupped her wan face in both hands. "I'll take care of you," he promised, his voice a rough growl. Olivia didn't seem to mind. A glimmer of blue washed into the turbulent gray sea of her eyes. "I know," she whispered.

He made her lie down with her good cheek resting on his leg. "Hold on, little one."

The doctor tried. The nurses tried. Sergeant McClary, interrupted at his breakfast by Jake's call, tried to convince Olivia to arrange for Maria to direct the wedding. Grimly amused, Jake watched from his unmovable stance against a wall in the county hospital emergency room while Olivia wielded her own version of Sinclair power.

"I don't have a concussion," she reminded the disgruntled physician. "I can manage the headache, especially if these pills work like you promised."

Outflanked, the doctor stuffed his stethoscope in the pocket of his white lab coat. "Everybody's different, of course, so I can't say for sure."

"But if they do work, you promised they wouldn't make me drowsy."

"Not supposed to." He shook his head. "You're doing the Judith Wells wedding, aren't you? I've known her since she was knee-high to a grasshopper. The wife and I planned to attend, so I reckon if you have a problem, at least I'll be handy."

That was the doctor.

Then the police officer started in. "Now, Ms. Sinclair, you know the more you expose yourself out in public, the better target you are. What if it's a bullet next time, instead of a brick? You have a capable assistant, so if I was you, I'd stay somewhere else for a day or two, 'til the boys and I have a little time to trace the car. You're sure about the driver?"

"Female, with short gray hair," Olivia repeated patiently. "It's not much, I know, but I had enough time between regaining consciousness and Mr. Donovan's arrival to sift it through my memory. I'm pretty good with details like that." She smiled. "I have to be."

"But you will at least move in with someone for a while? They've gotten personal now, ma'am. This is assault, a little more serious than malicious mischief."

Jake shouldered himself away from the wall. He'd had enough. "I'll take care of her," he announced in the tone of voice that never failed to produce the desired result.

It worked this time, too—with everyone except Olivia. Within five seconds the small emergency room of the county hospital had emptied, with polite farewells, advice, and shaking heads disappearing out the door.

Olivia, looking mulish, gingerly slid off the examining table. "You had no right to do that. It embarrassed me, and now they all think we're—" she stumbled, then finished defiantly—"involved."

"We are," Jake stated without cracking a smile, though he knew from Olivia's uneasy squirming that he'd successfully communicated his intent. He glanced down at his watch. "We can talk about it on the way to church. It's almost ten, and you're going to have enough trouble calming your two guardian angels as it is."

"If you're referring to Rollie and Maria, I prefer 'guardian angels' to 'spear-hurling Amazon bodyguards,'" Olivia grumbled, though she didn't resist the hand Jake slipped beneath her elbow. She fretted and muttered all the way to the car. "You called Maria to bring me some clothes, didn't you? I hope they fit okay . . . I have an image to maintain . . . we're the same size, I think—"

The county hospital was twenty miles away. Jake had to suppress the urgent desire to keep on driving, forcefully abducting Olivia like a marauding Viking and stashing her in the lodge in British Columbia with Garrick. Since he knew Olivia would never consent to that maneuver, he headed the car back toward Barley.

He thought she'd finally quieted down—until they turned onto the interstate. "Jake," she began, "I need to thank you before I say anything else."

"You already have. Don't you remember? At least every third sentence all the way over here." He grinned across at her. "It was my pleasure, ma'am. I'm just grateful the damage wasn't any worse than a huge bruise and a headache."

"I'll survive."

She didn't comment on the outcome of any future attacks, and, for the time being, Jake decided to play along. Timing, he knew, was everything, and right now, Olivia needed to pull herself together so she could marry off two kids with her professional persona intact. Deciding that teasing would put both of them in a lighter mood, Jake was mentally sifting through approaches when Olivia shoved him headfirst off a cliff.

"Jake . . . I don't know how to say this, and the circumstances aren't what I'd choose, but I need to say it and get it over with. Now. We—we can't be involved. Ever. On any level." He heard her swallow before continuing in a rapid, desperate monotone. "I just had to tell you now, especially after that little incident back at the hospital. It's impossible—all of it. I know I'm not a very good example, but I *am* a Christian, and I just can't handle a relationship with a man who only mentions God's name as a swear word."

Jake continued to drive without speaking until he knew his response wouldn't send Olivia scrambling for cover, or tumbling into another panic-driven trance. "Is that your only excuse?" he finally asked. "You sure you're not comparing me to your father?"

"Your resemblance to my father is and was only superficial," Olivia promised, sounding sincere but unutterably weary. "I at least settled that in my mind last night. You wield tremendous power, and you're the most exciting, disturbing man I've ever known." Out of the corner of his eye, Jake saw her lift her hand to her head, then drop it limply back in her lap. "But, as you pointed out almost from the first, you certainly play a lot more vicious hardball than I can in the game of life. That includes a deeply held dislike and mistrust of the Christian faith, and I just can't risk that—"

"I promised you last night I'd never hurt you like that again." He knew he sounded harsh, cutting, but he felt as if he were at the bottom of a pile of three-hundred-pound linebackers.

"I know." Her voice trembled for the first time. "I believe you . . . now. But, Jake, when all is said and done, you still hold all my beliefs, my faith, in contempt. I struggle enough as it is, trying to be a good Christian. I just can't—" her voice broke, and her head drooped—"can't risk it. I know you wouldn't mean to, but you'd end up destroying me."

"I've never understood why people set such store by a God who does nothing but promote fear and guilt and shame. There's no freedom in a miserable life of constant penance, endless rules and regulations, always waiting for God to drop the other shoe." He glared straight ahead at the concrete ribbon of road. "I grew up in an emotional jail like that . . . and hell couldn't be any worse. Olivia . . . help me understand. I need you in my life. If God is part of the price, then at least figure out a way to make the Christian life more palatable."

For a long time Olivia didn't respond, but Jake was struggling with ego-bruising battles of his own, so he didn't force the issue. A second swift glance assured him that, at least physically, Olivia seemed to be recovering. She sat straighter and some of her normal color had returned. He couldn't see the injured side of her face, which was just as well. Confronted with such graphic evidence of her vulnerability, he might have given up the battle then and there.

And lost the war.

Two miles from Barley, Olivia spoke again. "I didn't know my Christian faith came across like that."

"Like what?" he asked evenly.

"Like God is nothing but a God of wrath, or a harsh, small-minded jailer, gloating over the helplessness of all His inmates."

Jake shrugged and narrowed his eyes in thought. "Ever since I met you, your whole purpose in life has revolved around earning forgiveness for your father. You claim that's what Jesus did to pay for the sins of man, and you're only trying to follow His example." They entered the Barley city limits and Jake slowed the car practically to a crawl. He had maybe five more minutes.

"Well, I confess I've never had any use for Christianity," he went on, "because I've known many more miserable Christians than contented ones. It strikes me as a little contradictory that you're still trying to do for your father what Jesus is supposed to have already done. He died for everyone, if I understand it right, and that would have to include your father, no matter how despicable he might have been—" In the silence that followed, Olivia could hear her heart pounding. But Jake wasn't through. "It would have been up to *him* to make his peace with God, not you."

"Turn right at the next street," Olivia directed in a barely audible voice.

Two minutes later the church appeared. Frustration curdling his insides, Jake turned into the parking lot and pulled up beside Rollie's van. He switched off the ignition and turned to Olivia. She gazed back at him with the stricken self-awareness of a child caught stealing cookies.

Jake set his jaw. "If my teammates were right years ago about the role Jesus played, I'd have to say it's not God who's put you behind bars, Olivia. You've done it to yourself."

# thirteen

*Olivia is one classy lady,* Jake thought to himself, *and I'm was one messed-up guy.*

He watched her tolerate the ranting and raving of her friends long enough to calm them down, reassure them she would be fine, just fine. Then, looking unbelievably refreshed and confident in a borrowed dress, she quietly set Rollie to work and sent Maria off to the store.

With steadfast serenity, she ignored Rollie's questions as well as the gaping stares of the florist, photographer, and various other folk madly milling about. Over the next few hours—in spite of the fact that one side of her face looked like the aftermath of a barroom brawl—Olivia superintended the transformation of the quiet sanctuary into a lovely setting for the upcoming nuptials.

As a noticed but largely ignored bystander, Jake hovered in the background, so proud of this woman he wanted to stake a very public claim . . . yet so hurt, angry, and confused, he wanted to head for the mountains alone to lick his wounds. He still couldn't believe she'd given him the bum's rush because he didn't share her twisted, torturous views on God.

"Hello. I'm Michael Carmody, the minister here at First Street Methodist."

Jake turned to face a comfortable-looking man wearing a gray suit and surprisingly fashionable tie. Calm assessing eyes behind a pair of wire-rimmed glasses waited for

Jake to respond. Slowly he lifted a hand. "Jake Donovan."

"Are you part of the wedding party?"

"No way. I came with Olivia Sinclair, the busy little conductor over there talking to the organist."

"Ah, yes. Olivia. A lovely young woman who seems to be suffering greatly."

Struck both by the comment as well as the note of deep concern, Jake studied the older man a moment, frowning. "The doctor promised it's not a concussion, and he gave her some pills to help the headache," he offered neutrally.

"I wasn't referring to her physical discomfort," the pastor returned. Head canted slightly to one side, fingers idly stroking the underside of his chin, his gaze moved from Jake to Olivia. "A time or two, when you're not watching her, I've seen her look your way with the kind of soul-sick pain that would make the angels weep." To Jake's astonishment, one of Carmody's hands warmly gripped his shoulder. "They don't need me until two o'clock, so right now I'm sort of in the way no matter where I stroll. I think you're in the same boat, so . . . my office is just down the hall, away from the teeming hordes. Care to join me?"

The last thing, the very *last* thing Jake needed was a meddling, Bible-thumping preacher spouting off pious phrases. On the other hand—

"Sure, why not?" He shrugged, following Carmody and wondering if he'd finally gone round the bend for good.

A quiet oasis, the wood-paneled office was lined on two walls with floor-to-ceiling bookcases, the shelves full to overflowing. Sunlight streamed through a window onto the restful burgundy carpet. Off to one side a loveseat and two matching chairs surrounded a low table centered with a vase of cheerful yellow daffodils.

The preacher took one of the chairs, gesturing Jake toward the other. Ignoring the invitation, Jake prowled the room, reading some of the book titles, his skin crawling.

"Care for some coffee? Wedding punch?" Behind the glasses, brown eyes twinkled. "They're setting up the reception in our fellowship hall, and I reckon I could sneak us a couple of cups."

"No, thanks." Jake's eye fell on a worn Bible lying open on the table, next to the daffodils. With a sense of deep foreboding, he sat down. "Have you known Olivia very long?"

"She's done two weddings here, but I don't know her well. She's not a member of this church. And you?"

Okay, so he'd known when he came in here the guy would try to pick his brain, then start delivering sermons. If Jake objected . . . well, all he had to do was tell the preacher to take a hike. On the other hand, his best hope of understanding Olivia might be found with this man, who sat there watching Jake with the kindest pair of eyes he'd ever seen in his life.

"I've known her a couple of months now," Jake finally answered. Abruptly, he decided to see just what it took to rattle the Reverend Michael Carmody's cage. "I want her," he stated baldly, investing as much crudeness in the phrase as he could manage.

"I know," the preacher replied with a smile, almost knocking Jake out of the chair. "Don't look so surprised. You make it very obvious, you know—at least to me. Tell me—" he leaned forward—"does Olivia return your feelings?"

Jake couldn't remember the last time he'd blushed, but

he could feel the heat burning all the way to the back of his skull. Maybe he ought to blister the man's ears, but good, with some of the choice phrases he'd learned over the years ... but, no. He was a grown man, not a squirming adolescent boy who needed his mouth washed out with Aunt Sophy's lye soap.

Clenching his jaw, hands flexing on the chair arms, Jake met Carmody's gaze. "I think so, but she told me just before we arrived here that she doesn't want to see me anymore because I'm not a Christian." Rage and frustration and hostility boiled up and over, propelling him to his feet. He stood over the preacher and all but snarled. "So here's your chance. Don't you want to 'share the Good News?' 'Take me down the Roman road?' Convince me I need to be 'washed in the blood so I'll be saved?'"

"Sounds to me as if you've heard those words enough. From Olivia?"

*Did nothing spook this man?* "She knows better. Besides, she's so caught up being a martyr for her father, she hasn't had time to try her luck reforming *me* yet."

"A martyr for her father? Can you clarify that for me?" He held up a hand. "And no, I'm not asking you to divulge confidences or feel any more awkward than you already do." He watched Jake with a steady, unflappable compassion that all of a sudden reminded Jake of Garrick, except two more dissimilar men he'd never met. "Something's eating at you, son, isn't it? If you need to talk, why not give me a try? I promise not to back you into corners or preach any sermons."

Jake collapsed into the chair, propping elbows on knees, and resting his head in his hands. "I've never had much use for religion, or people who call themselves Christians," he confessed. Then he lifted his head. "But I've never met anyone like you. Or Olivia. And I guess you might say I'm about to go crazy. Listen, Reverend or Doctor or—"

"Mike'll do just fine, son."

"Mike, then. You know a lot about this stuff, right?" He waved his hand toward the Bible.

"Some. Most days I learn how little I really do know."

Jake ignored the dry note of humor. It reminded him too much of Olivia. "Tell me why God would take a beautiful woman of poise and charm and compassion, and ruin her life by making her atone for the cruelty of her father?"

For the first time surprise flashed across the preacher's face. "God *wouldn't*," he responded instantly, firmly. "He doesn't work like that."

Jake's hands lifted and fell. "Not according to Olivia. She claims she has to go around making people forgive her father, so that she can be free. 'Right with God,' she put it once." He snorted. "Doesn't make sense to me. I don't think I've ever met a woman less 'free' than Olivia. And yet she's so committed to Christ she'll throw away any chance we might have, just because I'm not willing to shackle myself in those kinds of chains."

Lines of concern deepened in Mike's face, and the twinkle in his eyes was replaced by a small but intense flame. "I think," he began carefully, "that what we have here is a gigantic misinterpretation of God's Word . . . on both your parts. Let me make sure I understand—Olivia is trying to pay for something her father did? Yet she claims to be a Christian?"

"You got it. I know all about how Jesus died for

mankind's sins. Could probably quote a few verses if I wanted to take the time to remember them. But when I try to point that out to Olivia, she just trots out this garbage about all the shame and guilt she feels because of who her father was." Mike looked blank so Jake obliged, too deeply involved now to care about Olivia's sensibilities. "Alton Sinclair. Chief loan officer and vice president of Fidelity Bank in Logan County. A twentieth-century Scrooge with a healthy dollop of Rasputin tossed in. Real charmer. He died in January. According to Olivia, she, her mother, and Sinclair's brother were the only three who attended his funeral. Not even the other two kids bothered to come. Olivia's the youngest and, for whatever reason, has taken on the burden of convincing people to forgive her old man's heinous deeds."

"Sounds to me as if Olivia is the one who needs to forgive her father."

"You're welcome to try to convince her."

Mike shook his head. "Forgiveness has to come from the heart, and only God can change hearts, son. That's a lesson every pastor learns, some of us the hard way. Now . . . take yourself."

Jake sat up, all of a sudden feeling very uneasy. "What about me?"

"Don't look so nervous. I just wanted to ask you a question." After a moment Jake gave a curt nod, and Mike leaned forward, his gaze unswerving, full of that disconcerting compassion. "Who is it *you* need to forgive for so poisoning your mind against God that all you see—like Olivia—is judgment, and none of His love?"

Olivia signaled the organist, then slipped back into the small side room at the back of the church, where a nervous bride and three bridesmaids waited. Seconds later Rollie appeared with the father of the bride—Rollie bustling, efficient, and Mr. Wells, more nervous than his daughter and all three bridesmaids put together.

"Everything's ready," Rollie whispered to Olivia. Her gaze settled on Olivia's swollen, hideously discolored forehead and cheek. "I do hope none of the other guests catches sight of you. That's why *I'm* here helping, remember?"

Judy, radiant in spite of bridal jitters, slipped a careful arm about Olivia and hugged her, engulfing Olivia in rustling taffeta and the heady spice of gardenia blossoms. "I can't thank you enough for being here, when we all know how dreadful you feel."

"And *look*," Olivia added, touching her cheek and wincing. At least the doctor's pills had eased the headache. "Now, remember...smile! You're giving yourself to the wonderful, loving man God picked out just for you. Not only that, but your wedding has been skillfully organized by the best consultant service in three states! Now how on earth could you keep from smiling?"

A gust of light laughter rippled through the room, and everyone relaxed. As the last of the guests were seated, Olivia quietly positioned herself in back, by the last pew. "Here we go," she whispered moments later, sending the first bridesmaid down the aisle to the stirring strains of the processional.

And none of them—not even Rollie—suspected that, deep inside, Olivia's heart was slowly breaking into a million pieces.

# fourteen

When Olivia finally dragged herself outside the church a little past four-thirty, Jake was sitting on the hood of his car, waiting. She hesitated, and he slid down, walking toward her with lazy, catlike grace. In the golden afternoon sunlight his hair gleamed like the satin sheen of a black tuxedo lapel.

Suddenly nervous, Olivia darted a swift glance about the almost deserted lot. "Where's Rollie, or should I ask?"

Jake paused a few feet away, watching Olivia with the unswerving concentration of a falcon hovering over a rabbit hole. "With some—persuasion, shall we say?—I sent her on her way. You and I have some unfinished business."

For hours Olivia had been dictating the movements of excited, malleable girls and awkward men, looking sheepish and uncomfortable in the rental tuxedos. Standing before her now in faded jeans and chambray shirt, Jake bore about as much resemblance to that crowd as a bubbling brook to Niagara Falls.

But Olivia knew she might as well try to contain Niagara with a teaspoon as to try and tell Jake Donovan anything. She tried anyway. "There's no need," she told him, starting down the steps. "I'm exhausted, and my face feels like a block of concrete. Jake, please, can't you just accept what I told you this morning?"

"You really are tired, to ask a ridiculous question like

that." Humor danced across his face. "Want me to carry you to the car?"

A flowing warmth swooped through Olivia in a groundswell, turning her stomach in a flip-flop. Her traitorous body easily conjured up the heady sensation of relaxing into Jake's strong, protective arms. *No way*, she opened her mouth to say, but "Yes," floated out instead.

Something flickered behind the gray eyes watching her so closely, and a deep chuckle wrapped around her heart as Jake's arms encircled her aching body. "You're always surprising me, sweetheart." He picked her up carefully, holding her close. "Here I am, geared for a battle royal, and you surrender without even lifting your sword."

"I'm too tired for fancy word games." She relaxed against him and closed her eyes, and tried not to think at all. "Jake, this is all wrong, and you're only going to make things worse."

"You'll feel better after we eat, and you take a nap." He placed her in the passenger seat, fastened her seat belt, then dropped a warm kiss on Olivia's drooping mouth. "Smile for me. It's not the end of the world."

"I wish you'd revert to your former intimidating self. I can fight that better." *Olivia, what are you saying?* She might as well send him an engraved announcement of her feelings.

"I don't want us to fight. I want us to communicate." He slid in beside her and started the car. "And, Olivia, I'll tell you right up front I had an extremely interesting conversation with Mike Carmody while you were playing Madame Wedding Director earlier today." His voice was soft, friendly—and implacable.

"Oh?" Headache and fatigue forgotten, Olivia sat up in

the seat. She stared out the window, wondering where Jake was taking her, since they were heading back toward the interstate. "What about?"

"Lots of things. Like you, and me, and you and me. Like you and your father. Like—" he hesitated as if searching for words, and Olivia's head swiveled around. Jake, looking tentative? "Like a view of God so radically different from yours, from the one rammed down my throat when I was growing up, that I'm having trouble grasping it. I'd like to talk about it, if you're willing," he finished, very quietly.

If he'd slapped her face, Olivia couldn't have been more dumbfounded. Never, ever in all these last weeks had it occurred to her that Jake would be willing to openly discuss such a volatile subject. And after the way they'd parted this morning, when she'd pretty much closed all the doors . . . it was too much. "I don't understand." Her voice wobbled, sounding as weak and befuddled as her brain.

"I know. Rest now, and we'll talk about it after we get there and you have food and a nap." He reached across the seat to massage the taut muscles at the nape of her neck. "Close your eyes. Relax. We're going to work it out, I promise."

"But where—"

"Shh. You've been in charge all day, now it's my turn. Lean your head back and close your eyes. That's it. Ah—ah. No more questions. Rest, sweetheart—"

And because she was so tired, and so flummoxed, she gave up and did as she was told.

She woke when they stopped and Jake turned off the

engine. Dazed and groggy, face painfully stiff, Olivia blinked until her eyes focused on a small clapboard house. It looked somehow familiar. "Where are we?"

Jake came around and opened her door, leaning over. "Beth's. She'll be home in a couple of hours. I couldn't take you to your place because it wouldn't be safe, and I sure wasn't going to come any closer to your two—ah—guardian angels than I had to."

Olivia's spine stiffened. "I really am tired of repeating myself, but I refuse to allow the actions of a coward and a criminal to frighten me out of my own home."

Jake leaned over until his face was only inches away. "You misunderstand," he breathed, gray eyes holding her in a warm, intimate cocoon that paralyzed her breathing. "It's not the stalker I'm thinking about right now, little goose. It's what will happen if I'm alone with you . . . with no chance of interruption."

Olivia gasped. In an outraged flurry of motion, she yanked open the car door and practically fell out, face flaming. Jake—laughing deep in his throat—had to catch her by the waist to keep her from sprawling headlong into the grass. "Be careful you don't hurt your head any worse," he counseled, hauling her up by his side and setting her gently on her feet.

"Why did you say that to me?" she demanded, torn by the equally strong desires to kick him in the shin as hard as she could . . . and melt in a puddle at his feet. "I could never . . . I wouldn't!"

"You think so now, but remember what I told you in your shop? I have an idea that even *Christians* are human—"

This had gone quite far enough. Olivia's head snapped back and, hands on hips, she leveled a look at him that dried up his laughter quicker than snow melts in the hot sun. "Jake Donovan, I can only imagine what kind of women you've associated with in your life. I can further imagine what your response will be to what I'm about to say, but right now I—I just don't care!"

Olivia didn't have much of a temper, but the time or two in her life when something finally provoked her to wrath, she could rival a tornado while the fury lasted. And right now she was tired, hurting, and confused—totally incapable of maintaining any semblance of serenity. Jake's outrageous statement, uttered so confidently, sent the mercury straight over the top of the bulb.

"I will *not* let you do this to me! You can mock and make snide remarks about God and Christianity all you want, trot out all the clichés men and women in today's society use to justify their behavior. And don't think for one minute that, just because I haven't been around the block like you, means I don't know most of them." Olivia advanced, poking her finger against his chest, forcing him to retreat until he backed smack into the car. " 'Everybody's doing it,'" she mimicked in scathing sarcasm. " 'Who's it going to hurt if we both agree?' 'Hardly anybody waits until marriage anymore—' Does that cover most of it?"

"Olivia, I wasn't trying—"

"*Let me finish!*" Olivia roared, oblivious to her stiff face and the anvil pounding away in her skull. "I don't care *how* much I love you, Jake Donovan, I will *not* make love to any man except the man I marry. I may be the world's most messed-up Christian, but I do know the difference between right and wrong. Now leave me alone! Do you hear me?"

"I imagine the whole block can hear," Jake drawled, a

strange light kindling the gray eyes, turning them to molten silver.

Breathing hard, Olivia glared around, ready to blister any unfortunate soul careless enough to have wandered within earshot. Then she realized what she'd said, and her verbal tornado evaporated with an abrupt little poof. Her gaze met Jake's, and she closed her eyes. "What have I done?" she whispered. "Dear Lord, what have I done?"

She felt Jake's hands on her arms, tugging her toward him. "No!" She wrenched free, heart pounding. She wanted to run, hide, disappear for at least a hundred years.

"Don't do this, Olivia." He made no move to reach out again.

Rigid, eyes monitoring every muscle twitch, every breath he took, Olivia frantically willed herself to be calm, in control. Lift her chin and face him down. She wasn't the first woman in the world to make a fool of herself over a man, and she wouldn't be the last.

Jake leaned back against the car and forced himself to relax. Very slowly, very casually he stuffed one hand in the front pocket of his jeans, the other on the car door. He had to be very careful. "Listen to me," he ordered, keeping his voice low, calm. "Olivia? Are you listening?"

Jerkily, she nodded once.

*So far, so good.* He tried a coaxing smile. "I didn't know you had such a fierce temper. I'll have to be more careful in the future not to provoke it."

Olivia's expression didn't change by so much as the flicker of an eyelash.

*Hmm,* Jake thought. He studied her flushed face, feeling pretty breathless himself. Over the years he'd enjoyed the attentions of a lot of forgettable women, some of whom had whispered honeyed words of love to his face, while mentally counting his money. And if they didn't care about his financial assets, all they wanted was a good time. To them, he was nothing but a challenge, untamable, like the big game he'd tracked a few times in the wilderness.

In all this time, Jake had never really trusted the love of any other person outside of his sister Beth. And that included the first and last woman he had ever asked to be his wife.

"Did you know I was married once?" Ah. That little revelation elicited a response. Olivia blinked owlishly, throat muscles working. But at least she was listening now. "I was only nineteen. My wife died giving birth to our child." He'd never confessed the deeply buried secret to another person other than Sherm, who Jake knew would carry the information to the grave.

Now, desperate as he'd never been, even all those years ago, Jake unlocked his soul to Olivia. He owed her some indication of reciprocal trust, even though right now he realized her temper-induced declaration had been unintentional. The trouble was, he couldn't look into Olivia's eyes and share the disgusting story. He turned, staring over the top of the car, and began to talk.

"Maribel was seventeen, and both of us were wild as weasels. I was on my way to the pros, and one weekend we drove up to West Virginia and got hitched. Then I left for spring training. And Maribel realized she didn't want to leave home, after all." Why wouldn't Olivia say something? *Please, God, don't let her shut me out.* He found himself praying for the first time in his life—and meaning it.

"I'd come back when I could, try to convince her. The

'convincing' usually turned into a full-blown argument. Then she got pregnant—" Jake rested his arms on the roof of the car and closed his eyes. "By that time she hated me. And she hated the idea of having the baby. She refused to see a doctor, take care of herself. The town where we lived was two hours from the nearest hospital. She went into labor one night while I was playing a game in New York. By the time I made it home, she was dead . . . along with our son. They told me she died . . . screaming how much she hated us both—"

Behind him came the sound of a muffled sob. Jake spun, and Olivia hurled herself into his arms. "I'm sorry," she choked, tears streaming down her cheeks. "Jake, I'm so sorry. That must have been terrible. . . no wonder you—" She buried her head in his shoulder.

Stunned, Jake struggled to cope with Olivia's abrupt turnabout. Holding her close, automatically rubbing her shoulders and back, fractured thoughts and half-formed sentences crashed drunkenly around his brain. She was crying . . . for him? "Please stop, baby. You're killing me—and probably your head. It's okay, I promise." He kissed her hair, inhaling the piquant aroma of Olivia's perfume—and a lingering antiseptic scent from the medicine daubed on her face at the hospital.

"I'm sorry I told you," he soothed. "I just wanted you to understand, wanted you to know you can trust me not to take advantage of you just because—" *Shut up, Donovan, before you blow it even worse.* He gently tugged the hair at the back of her neck, forcing Olivia to lift her head. Carefully, carefully his hand cupped the uninjured cheek, thumb rubbing the tears away.

Then, helpless against the waterfall of feelings, he

began to kiss her, soft, urgent kisses covering her eyes, her
forehead, her mouth. In between kisses, he whispered
nonsensical phrases, broken endearments, desperate to
absorb her pain—and drown out his own.

With an inarticulate moan, Olivia's hands slid around
the back of his neck and she clung to him so desperately
that something deep inside Jake shifted, then melted away.
And he knew that—no matter what she said—Olivia
Sinclair loved him. Not just from her head, or her wildly
swinging emotions, but from the heart.

*Dear God,* Jake prayed, *if You're anything like Mike
Carmody said, I need help. Really bad, really quick.*

# fifteen

March blew into April, and Olivia's face healed. There were no further attacks on either her person or her possessions. The police continued to patrol her neighborhood regularly, and every few days one would check in at The Bower.

Rollie left for a week-long trip to Raleigh, Richmond, and Atlanta to check on new suppliers. Maria insisted that Olivia phone her every evening at bedtime and in the morning before she left for work. Tired of protesting, Olivia complied.

Days were checked off with clockwork efficiency. She continued to volunteer at Sherm's Shelter, and one rainy Saturday afternoon, she again accompanied Beth on her weekend visit to Davy.

Neither of them had heard from Jake for close to two weeks.

"What do you think Jake wants out of life?"

Beth stopped right in the middle of the corridor leading to Davy's room, staring up at Olivia in astonishment. "Why on earth would you ask me that now? Here? You don't speak ten words the whole drive over, and now that we're on Davy's doorstep, you ask a mind-boggling question like what I think my brother wants out of life?"

Always too thin, too pale, and too tired, Beth nonetheless manifested a bedrock kind of upbeat endurance Olivia envied. She was also never too tired to broadcast whatever was on her mind.

Olivia ducked her head to hide a flicker of amusement. "I haven't had the courage to bring it up before now," she replied. "And I also decided if I gave you time to think, you'd just manufacture a plausible answer you figured would be more palatable to my ears than the truth."

Both women stepped aside for a wheelchair-bound elderly man being pushed by an orderly. The orderly, a whippy-looking young man with one earring, flashed them a cheeky grin. To Olivia's surprise, Beth blushed.

"What was *that* about?"

Nervously fingering her purse, Beth shrugged. "Oh . . . that's Ray. He's tried to flirt with me a time or two, once in front of Davy. Nothing serious, but the last time I was here, Davy tried to imitate Ray . . . and put his arm around my waist, too." She smiled sadly. "That's the first and last gesture of affection I've had from my husband in three years."

"I'm sorry." Olivia hugged her briefly. "I have a nerve, don't I, picking your brain about Jake. You're in an impossible situation, Beth. I think I admire you about as much as anybody I know."

They reached the door to Davy's room, and Beth flashed her a grateful look. "Thanks, Olivia. For whatever it's worth, what you're doing—coming here with me, I mean—means a lot to me. Jake thinks you have a lot of class, and I'd have to agree." She opened the door. "Hi, Davy Crockett! Look who's back for a visit today."

Davy had been sitting on the floor beneath the window, playing with some plastic cowboys and Indians Olivia had brought on her last visit. At Beth's cheerful greeting, he looked up, two tiny figures clutched in each hand. A tall gangling man with tousled strawberry blond hair and a wide grin, the look of vapid ingenuousness never failed to chill Olivia's blood. *How in the world does Beth stand it?*

She followed Davy's wife—wife!—across the floor and knelt with her beside Davy. "Hi, Davy." She forced herself to take his hand and pump it up and down.

Davy's pale green eyes smiled vacantly up at her. "Hi." He seldom spoke beyond simple greetings, and an occasional giggle. The young man who had once dreamed of running his own small-engine repair shop . . . now played on the floor with plastic baby toys. Olivia never knew whether to cry—or rage—at both her father and Davy.

Watching Beth sitting cross-legged on the floor, quietly sharing the events of her day as if Davy understood every word, Olivia had to quell an uprush of tears. Ever since Jake left almost a month ago, her emotions had seesawed violently. She hadn't felt like crying like this since she was a lonely teenager.

"Ah, love!" Maria would wave her hands and look superior. "Crying comes with the territory, kiddo."

With determined cheerfulness, Olivia dug into the huge floral totebag she'd brought along. Dragging out a coloring book and box of crayons, she knelt on the floor, holding them out. "Look, Davy, I've brought you a present." She and Beth spent the next few minutes coloring with Davy, and when he lost interest, Olivia laid everything aside. "I'll wait in the lobby," she told Beth.

She always left Beth alone for the last thirty minutes or so of their visit. It was in these moments that she knew Beth tried to talk to Davy as if he were still a responsible man—husband, provider, protector, friend. Olivia might feel she herself needed to earn forgiveness, help pay for her father's sins, but she could not bear to witness this—this travesty of a relationship.

*What would I do if Jake turned into a living mockery of a man?* The very idea was a torture. Would she still accept and love him as Beth did Davy . . . or was she her father's daughter, after all, with shallow, selfish emotions that could be turned on and off like a water faucet?

Deep in thought, Olivia wandered back down the bright, sterile corridor to the lobby. In the long run, the depth of her love for Jake might be totally irrelevant. They had made no permanent commitment to each other, nor had Jake voiced aloud any passionate avowals of love for her.

In fact, when he told her goodbye last time, he'd been almost offhand, preoccupied. "I think we both have some serious thinking to do, and being apart might make it easier right now." Olivia wasn't sure what kind of serious thinking a man indulged in while white water rafting, but with Jake, one never knew.

"I looked up one of the guys on my team who claimed he was a Christian," Jake had said in that same farewell conversation. "It's pretty humbling, I have to admit. I used to ridicule Tony, claim he was no better than the rest of us. He always agreed, said he *wasn't* better . . . just saved. When we talked the other day, I saw how wrong I was years ago. He might not be better, but he *is* different." Then Jake had cupped her chin. "He doesn't wallow in shame, Olivia. In fact, he reminded me a bit of this guy I met in Canada. And I think . . . I think I want to know more. And I think *you* need to take a look at a few things, too."

Then he'd kissed her. "Throw out the old rule book, little one. We both might be surprised."

Right, Olivia thought now. If she believed that, she

might as well move to New York and open a shop on Fifth Avenue.

Beth joined her forty minutes later.

"Any luck?" Olivia asked, and as always Beth shook her head.

After each visit with Davy, Olivia had noticed that it took Beth quite a while to return to her *own* reality. On the drive back to her home in Granite Falls, Beth would sit motionless in her seat, head back and eyes closed, drained and limp as week-old cut flowers. Then, stretching, shrugging her shoulders as if to slip off the unbearable emotional weight, she returned to her normal gregarious, artless self.

Today she surprised Olivia. "I talked to Davy about your question. Remember . . . you were wondering what Jake wants out of life? Davy was a big help." She grinned across at Olivia. "He let me talk without interrupting until I sorted out some thoughts."

"Beth, I didn't mean—"

"If you apologize again for what you perceive as your guilt over the way *my* life turned out, I'll open the door and jump out while you're driving sixty. Now . . . about my big brother." She rolled the window down a little, took a deep breath. "We both know one of the things he wants is you."

Olivia shifted uneasily, and Beth laughed. "Don't worry, I won't embarrass you like I did the day you'd been walloped by a brick, when I came home from work early and surprised the two of you right there in the driveway—"

Olivia scowled with mock ferocity. "Maybe it *would* be a good idea for you to jump out of the car."

"Okay, okay." Beth fiddled with the buttons on her

blouse a moment, then threw up in her hands in a gesture of surrender. "You and your Christian principles have tied Jake up in knots, and you know it. It's tying me in knots, too. It blows me away that Jake's starting to talk like that himself. This is the man who used to run off to another *continent* if someone even suggested he might benefit from poking his head through a church door once a year or so." She gave a wry grin.

"And it was the kiss of death for any woman to even hint at the possibility of a long-term 'commitment.' Now... *now* my brother not only goes around talking like a preacher, he's making weird noises about settling down. I know he doesn't plan to kiss you off like he has all the other women who've made fools of themselves over him the last ten years or so. No offense."

"None taken." Olivia sighed. Sometimes Beth's ruthless candor could be as hard-hitting as Jake's.

"Nope," Beth continued, "Jake's not ready to write you off. But as to how that fits in with what he plans to do in the long run, your guess is as good as mine, Olivia. Jake's been a rolling stone and a rootless wanderer all his life—even before Maribel." She shook her head. "I still can't believe he told you about that. Between that—and catching him reading the Bible that last week before he left —about the only thing I know for sure is that he's changing."

There went her heart again, cartwheeling like her stomach. Olivia passed her tongue over suddenly dry lips. "You really do think he's changing?"

Beth nodded. "Yep. He keeps mumbling about this different view of God, and how maybe Jesus was more than just a reason for Christians to feel guilty all the time.

You know, it's hard enough trying to understand your crackpot desire to pay for everything your father did. But now Jake's spouting off all these weird ideas about how Jesus was really God's plan to make everybody feel *free*, not guilty. I don't know what on earth is going on between the two of you, Olivia, but it's not like any relationship with a woman he's ever had before. Like I said, he's changing."

Looking unsettled and uncomfortable, Beth abruptly leaned forward and flipped on the radio. "Used to be all Jake wanted out of life was another mountain to climb. Now I don't have a clue as to what he *really* wants."

Rollie, Maria—and Sergeant MacClary—were waiting in Olivia's driveway when she pulled up a few hours later. So many horrific possibilities stormed through Olivia's brain, the car almost plowed into the back of the police cruiser.

She threw open the door. "What is it? What's happened? The Bower?"

"Now, don't go pitching a hissy fit," Rollie interjected as Olivia skidded to a halt in front of them. "Everything's fine, except we're about to perish from boredom and thirst, waiting for you to stroll along home."

Rolling her eyes at the older woman, Maria took pity on Olivia. "Jake called," she announced baldly, grinning at Olivia's flabbergasted silence. "That's not the end of it. Next he called Sergeant MacClary." She nodded to the policeman. "This, now, is the kicker—Olivia, he wants you to join him."

"In Georgia," Rollie added. "But not tempting death in

some little rubber boat going down the Chattooga. He wants you to join him at the home of some friends of his."

Sergeant MacClary, looking resigned but relieved, finally added his two cents. "Since you continue to refuse to move in with someone else a while, this would at least provide a mite more safety while me and the boys close in on our suspect."

Olivia caught her breath. "You found the woman driving the car?" she asked, ignoring for the moment Jake's high-handed machinations. "Why haven't you told me?"

"We-ell . . . I'm telling you now. But don't go getting too excited. We're hopeful, but we still have to check on a few things." To Olivia's growing frustration, he wouldn't add anything further except to say, "It would make my supper settle easier if you took a nice little trip for a week."

Tapping her foot, Olivia's gaze raked all three of them. "I appreciate the concern, but Jake had no right to go behind my back like this. Besides, this is our busiest season. I couldn't possibly go traipsing off in the woods somewhere right now." *Even though I'd love to just toss it all to the wind to be with Jake, no matter how it was arranged. . . .*

Hands on hips, Maria thrust out a stubborn chin. "Oh, yes, you can. Rollie and I have talked it over, and we've figured out a way to manage everything for one week without you to oversee, remind, plan, and otherwise check off blocks in your planner. So you're going and that's that."

"Olivia, you could use a vacation and you know it," Rollie chimed in. "You haven't taken any time off in at least four years."

Olivia wanted to pull her hair in exasperation and sheer disbelief. "What is this? You're all practically throwing me at the same man you threatened to boil in oil only weeks ago—"

At least Rollie had the good grace to look uncomfortable. Maria merely continued to smile like a gleeful matchmaker.

"Ah . . . can we talk about this inside, ladies?" Sergeant MacClary suggested, removing his cap and mopping his brow. "It's been a tad warm, waiting out here."

"Certainly." Olivia stalked up the path. "But I'm not going. I don't have time . . . it's simply out of the question."

## sixteen

Jake met her at Hartsfield International Airport in Atlanta.

They hadn't seen each other in over a month, and so much had happened Jake couldn't decide if the time had flown in microseconds or dragged in decades. In those weeks he'd found himself waking in the predawn hours, listening a while in the dark reverent hush of night—and almost feeling God's affirming, sustaining Presence. It was so real, so life-transforming, that now it was Jake's former restless, wandering spirit that seemed alien and distant.

He still had a lot to learn, of course.

And he had some explaining to Olivia to get out of the way first, before he shared anything else. Waiting for her plane, surrounded by the crush of seething humanity, Jake was sweating bullets.

Okay, so maybe he should have called her to make the arrangements, instead of ambushing her through Maria and Rollie. Originally, he had called Olivia's friends to enlist their aid on how best to approach Olivia, and to convince him that his intentions—to quote the time-honored chestnut—were entirely honorable this time.

Maria persuaded him to circumvent Olivia entirely. "Trust me," she urged. "She needs someone to dictate her life for a while. And though I never dreamed I'd be saying this, in spite of first appearances, I think you just might be the man for the job here. Oh . . . while you're at it, see if you can charm her into throwing away her daily planner. She's giving me and Rollie flying duck fits, organizing us to the point when she schedules what time we can blow our noses."

The intercom crackled to life, announcing the arrival of Olivia's flight. Jake jerked upright, pulse wild as the Chattooga River rapids. *You there, God? I hope so, since Olivia's just as likely to deck me as she is to kiss me.*

Beyond that, he wondered what Olivia's reaction would be when he did have the chance to share the unbelievable odyssey that had led him from the white water of his former life to the quiet streams King David talked about in his Book of Psalms. From a man who eschewed all ties to a man who was now committed to a lifelong relationship. A bonafide, one-to-one personal relationship with a Person whose reality Jake had spent a lifetime denying. As he'd done for days now, Jake searched his feelings, testing them. He still found mostly warmth and acceptance, while the residue of denial and panic continued to diminish.

Passengers from Olivia's flight began straggling through the door. Jake breathed deeply, forcing himself to be calm, watching from a spot off to the side where he could see Olivia before she saw him. When she finally appeared, clutching a huge floral tote in one hand and her briefcase-sized purse in the other, Jake's insides clenched in a sharp, exultant stab of sheer possessiveness. Whether Olivia was ready to admit it or not, she was his.

Then Jake looked into her face. *Okay, Donovan, put a lid on it, fella.* Her mouth was set, face chalky, her pupils so distended her eyes looked like two black pits. Jake shouldered his way through the crowd in a silent rush. "Olivia." Then he stood there, just drinking in the reality of her presence.

His silence met head-on Olivia's indomitable control. "Well . . . I'm here." He saw her fingers move convulsively, but her step didn't falter as she walked straight up to Jake—looking steadfastly over his right shoulder the whole time.

"I see that," Jake replied, suddenly feeling as tongue-tied and dull as a twelve-year-old schoolboy. "Now . . . let's get out of here. I hate airports."

"I need to make a phone call first."

Her brittle, too-calm facade was driving him mad, but Jake at least had found his temper easier to control lately. "You can find a phone in the main terminal. I'll show you," he managed just as politely.

He waited—torn between incredulity and impatience— while she called Maria at The Bower and spent twenty minutes delivering three pages of instructions she'd apparently written on the flight down. Jake began to see what Maria meant about that daily planner.

Finally, after receiving Maria's promise to call Olivia's mother, and to check in with Sergeant MacClary at least twice a week, Olivia hung up. She smoothed her hands over her jacket, then brushed her hair back and turned to Jake, still looking like a professional female on a business trip.

Jake wanted to ruffle her hair and to shuck her from the jacket like an ear of corn. "Do you need anything to eat?" he inquired instead, wincing inside at the barbed civility of his own voice. Olivia coolly shook her head; maybe instead of hair-ruffling and coat-shucking, he should toss her over his shoulder—or dump her right here in the middle of the airport and let her find her own way back home. As always, his and Olivia's reunions never went the way Jake planned.

"Give me your baggage claim." Slowly, Olivia retrieved it from her purse and held it out. Jake plucked it from her fingers—and felt as if he'd plunged his hand into a bucket of ice cubes.

Their eyes met, and Jake watched as before his eyes the prickly professional pose crumbled, then dissolved like a sack of wet sugar. He tucked the ticket in his pocket, gently relieved Olivia of the cumbersome tote, then enclosed her cold, trembling hands in his own. "You're afraid, aren't you? So much so you've turned into a block of ice, inside and out."

Lifting her hands, he gently blew his warm breath across the chilled fingers, seeing for the first time the lines of strain around her mouth, her eyes. "What is it, sweetheart? I know they couldn't have bullied you into coming if you were really that scared of facing me away from your own turf, so to speak."

She ducked her head, faint color seeping under her skin. "It's not just that," she finally muttered.

"Then what?" Jake prodded, hefting the ridiculous tote over one shoulder while his fingers continued to stroke her trembling hand and the inside of her wrist where the pulse fluttered like a trapped animal's. "I've . . . never flown before."

He couldn't have heard right. Letting the tote slide with a heavy thud to the ground, Jake took her by the shoulders and turned her toward him. "You've never flown? Not once in your entire life?"

"It's not a crime," she snapped, sounding cranky and belligerent and sheepish all at the same time.

Jake couldn't help it. He laughed, pulled her close and kissed her soundly, oblivious to the grinning passersby swarming past in an endless tide. "And here I was terrified your feelings toward me might have changed—" He kissed her again, bottling the protests. "Shh . . . lying's a sin, remember?"

That laughing aside earned him five minutes of stunned silence which carried them all the way down to the baggage claim area. Then, during the next irritating minutes of retrieving her single suitcase, the long walk to the Rover, and waiting to leave the car park, Olivia searched his features, would start to speak, then clamp her mouth shut again.

Not until they were headed north on the freeway did she finally manage to phrase a question, only it wasn't the one Jake had hoped for. "Is this yours?" she queried, gesturing to the Toyota Range Rover he drove. Apparently she still needed to reassess her faltering defensive line a while longer.

"Nope. Belongs to a friend of mine, Luke Farringer. That's where we're headed, by the way. He and his wife run an injured wildlife preserve a little over two hours north of here. You'll like them."

"You mean I'm not going to be screaming down a river in a little rubber raft or dangling off the side of a mountain on a rope the width of a clothesline?"

*Now that was vintage Olivia.* Jake felt his muscles relaxing, and a headache he hadn't even been aware of receded. "Well . . . I suppose I could arrange something, but I don't think you're quite ready to tackle 'Screaming Left Turn Rapids' or the 'Corkscrew' quite yet. As for climbing, maybe the hills behind the Farringers' place."

He flicked her a challenging grin. "I know lots of hidden, private spots to show you."

"A day or two ago, your sister threatened to jump out of my car while I was driving along at about sixty miles an hour," Olivia mused, finally relaxing her spine enough to rest against the seat. "That kind of talk makes me want to jump, too . . . and you're doing a little better than sixty."

*I love you.* He almost said the words aloud, but checked himself just in time. Jake had spent the last two weeks planning his moves carefully, as carefully as he planned his trips—methodically, down to the last detail, leaving nothing to chance. In that way, he and Olivia were very much alike. Jake smiled to himself. Soon, very soon, his lady-love would be discovering they had more in common than she could possibly have dreamed.

Luke and Cattleya Farringer lived on three hundred acres of some of the most beautiful land on God's earth. Jake loved to visit them in the spring, when the wooded hills were all decked out in every shade of green on the palette, and redbuds and rhododendron were bursting open in a riot of color. The melodious gurgle of the stream could be heard at the bottom of the meadow behind their house. Delicate yellow trillium magically sprouted between dew-wet tree trunks. Graceful deer visited in the meadow at dusk.

If Jake ever decided to settle down, it would be somewhere in the southern Appalachians in a place like this. If he settled down—

The Rover bounced its way up the winding dirt two-track road leading to the Farringers', and Jake waited to feel the old knee-jerk compulsion to head for the hills.

Out of the corner of his eye, he watched Olivia absorbing the peace and incredible beauty. Rolling the window down, she filled her lungs with the crisp, biting air of late afternoon. To his surprise, the only emotion registering with Jake was the consuming desire to have this woman with him—in a place like this.

*So . . . You really do make new creatures out of us.*

He tooted the horn as they rounded the last curve leading into the lush valley where Hope Hill sprawled under the shadow of the southern Appalachians. The track led right to the magnificent rambling old Victorian house Luke and Leya had spent the last seven years renovating.

At the sound of the horn, Joey Farringer and his usual assortment of animals spilled from the doors, off the wraparound porches, from under the porches. Across the yard Josh, Joey's twin brother, shimmied down a tree and scampered across the field like a chipmunk.

Olivia turned to Jake. "I've never seen anything more beautiful or . . . welcoming."

"I know exactly what you mean," Jake replied, his gaze resting on Olivia's wondering face. "Now, the two whirling dervishes approaching are Josh and Joey Farringer, five-year-old twins and occasional unholy terrors. Luke and Leya also take in foster kids. They've only got two at the moment because. Hi, Josh! How's it going, man?"

"You took forever to get here, Jake!" the child scolded. "I was the lookout, but I fell asleep." The blue-eyed urchin clambered up the side of the Rover, and Jake ruffled the silky brown hair. His brother, Joey, dashed up to join Joshua, the only distinguishing mark setting the twins apart, the scar on Josh's forehead from falling out of the tree last year. Jake knew the boy was proud of that scar because it matched one on his mother's cheek.

"Okay, guys, back off so I can introduce you to my friend Olivia." Leya appeared in the front door of the house, then started across with Marsha, the fifteen-year-old girl who'd only been here a couple of months. Jake reached for Olivia's hand. "You look like a missionary about to be sacrificed to the cannibals . . . which is a good metaphor, since Leya used to be a missionary."

Olivia took another deep breath of the fresh country air. Her fleeting smile disappeared, along with the faint wash of blue in her uncertain eyes.

Jake winked at the twins, then slid across the front seat to wrap an arm around Olivia and hug her close. He wanted badly to kiss her, but knew that would only embarrass her, so he nobly resisted temptation. Just. "Knowing you, within two days you'll have the whole place marching to your tune—including the twins. Maybe I'd better warn everyone while I have a chance."

This time her smile lingered.

Jake leaned over and opened her door as Leya and Marsha drew abreast. "Well, here she is at last, gals. Olivia Sinclair, meet Cattleya Farringer and Marsha."

"Welcome to Hope Hill, Olivia." Leya held out a slim brown hand. "Luke and I are delighted you're here. Luke should be along for dinner. He's down at the corral with Nails. Nails is our . . . foreman, I suppose you might say," she explained to Olivia. "He accompanied some mustangs from New Mexico six years ago and refused to leave. He's been here ever since."

Jake followed Olivia out her side of the vehicle, then swept Leya up in a careful embrace. She was seven months pregnant and thankfully healthy now, though Jake—like Luke—tended to treat her like one of the fragile orchids for which she'd been named. Her long red-gold hair was coiled in its usual neat coronet on top of her head, the smiling eyes deep pools of serenity. Luke Farringer is one lucky guy, Jake thought. Or rather, he checked himself, he's been greatly blessed by God.

To the world, the result might be the same. Jake, however, had learned that therein lay a world of difference.

# seventeen

A storm swept over the mountains that evening, deluging Hope Hill with torrential rain and sending booming thunder rolling down over the hills. Olivia helped Leya prepare a late supper for the adults, while Marsha and Ben, their other foster child, supervised the twins' bedtime preparations. Jake and Luke braved the weather to doublecheck all the animals.

"We have livestock in two barns and wild animals in a third barn a mile or so away," Leya explained while she and Olivia puttered about the kitchen. "We'll show you tomorrow. It's over a foothill, so the sounds of their calls won't upset the domesticated animals. Our latest pride and joy, though, is the enclosed bird sanctuary Luke finally finished last summer—about half a mile from here."

Lightning lit up the night sky seconds before a teeth-jarring thunderclap rattled the pots and pans hanging above the stove. Leya peered out the window, a tiny frown puckering her smooth brow. "That's probably where he and Jake are now. A ranger over on Springer Mountain brought us a golden eagle who'd been shot last month. It's so frustrating. . . . They're an endangered species, and the few left east of the Mississippi are only migratory." She gestured apologetically. "Sorry. I tend to jump right up on the soapbox." She handed Olivia a stack of mismatched plates from the cupboard, all of them unbreakable plastic.

"Luke's been spending most of his days there. And a lot of evenings, as you see."

Remembering the depth of worry in Luke Farringer's vivid blue eyes, Olivia nodded. "Your husband is—" she hesitated, uncertain of Leya's response if Olivia voiced her compliment.

Leya turned, her tranquil smile banishing all traces of concern. "I know. Don't worry, Olivia. I won't accuse you of making eyes at my husband if you want to tell me how divinely wonderful he is."

Laughing, Olivia colored. "That's not exactly how I was going to put it, but yes—he is wonderful. Especially with you. He's so loving, and—and gentle." *Like Jake has been on a few memorable occasions with me.* Hope and despair battled in her heart, and she turned away so Leya wouldn't notice.

Unfortunately, Leya was as perceptive as she was friendly. "Jake has shared a little of your past," she volunteered casually. "It's a wonder you let any man within a hundred miles."

Mortified, Olivia didn't say a word, and after a moment Leya pursued the topic with gentle determination. "My father and I didn't get along very well for a long time, but from what Jake shared about yours, my father is a saint by comparison. Please forgive Jake for talking about you, Olivia. It's just that he's needed a sounding board as well as a spiritual counselor these last couple of weeks and ... well ... he and Luke have a lot in common." She came and sat down in one of the kitchen chairs, massaging the small of her back. "Whew. Don't you dare let anyone know that sometimes it does feel good to put my feet up a few minutes."

Olivia barely heard her last words. "What did you mean about Jake needing a 'spiritual counselor?'" she asked, dropping down into a chair across from Leya, feeling dazed.

Leya pursed her lips, studying Olivia. "I think," she mused carefully, "maybe it would be better if you heard it from Jake."

At that moment Marsha sidled through the kitchen doorway. "The boys are in bed," she announced in her timid, whispering voice, "but I don't know how long they'll stay, with this storm. Ben let them each take one of Sauce's kittens if they promised not to get up. Was that okay?" She looked, Olivia thought sadly, as if she were waiting to be struck.

"If they can keep the kittens in bed without getting out themselves," Leya returned serenely. "Otherwise, Ben will have to take them to their mama in the cellar. You might also tell him that if he'll read to the twins a while, I'll reward him with some molasses crinkles tomorrow."

"Can I have some, too, Leya?"

"Of course you can, Marsha. Now come here and give me a hug. I'm feeling droopy and need a pick-me-up." Marsha's embrace barely lasted a half second before she scooted back out the kitchen door. She hadn't once looked at Olivia.

"Just a week ago she wouldn't have touched me at all," Leya observed with satisfaction. "Thank You, Lord, for Your healing hands."

*And yours and Luke's,* Olivia added to herself. She looked down at her own hands, clenched so tightly on the table that the skin was mottling. She wanted to heal people, too, but thus far had met with nothing but failure.

"Before Ben came to live with us, he thought the only kind of books in the world had pictures of naked women in them . . . and the child only eleven years old," Leya continued musing in her lovely soft voice. "It just makes my heart feel all 'squishy,' as the boys would say, when we can see the Lord healing these poor unhappy souls."

"I don't understand how you do it," Olivia suddenly exclaimed, words spewing forth as if she'd sliced open a festering boil. "The children, the animals . . . even this house . . . everything you and Luke touch seems to bloom. And you're always so—so full of joy . . . and peace. I'm a Christian, too, but compared to you, I feel like a Pharisee or something equally despicable! And no matter how hard I try, I end up making a mess of things!" *If you start crying, Olivia Sinclair, I will never forgive you.*

Suddenly, bright and violent as the lightning bolts outside, a shaft of inner illumination blazed across Olivia's mind. "Oh, dear God—" She stuffed a fist over her mouth. "That's my whole problem, isn't it? I hate myself, I hate my father, and that means God can't forgive me, either. I don't know what I'm going to do—"

Cattleya inched her chair around until she could wrap an arm about Olivia's rigid shoulders. "The first thing you're going to do is to stop comparing yourself," she chastised, giving Olivia a slight shake, "to me, or to anyone else. If the Lord wanted all of us to be the same, He'd have formed us with a cookie cutter!"

"Well, I know using Jesus as my example makes me look even worse," Olivia joked feebly, but the stinging pressure behind her eyes only intensified. Blinking hard and staring fixedly at her knotted hands, she would have run from the room except she had no place to run to except straight into a storm that mirrored the one raging in her soul.

"Olivia, did you know that—before this baby—I suffered two miscarriages? I almost died after the last one—" Olivia froze, jerking her head up to face the steady compassion blazing out of Leya's eyes. "The doctor told us I'd probably never carry another child full term . . . yet here I am—" She rubbed her rounded abdomen lovingly—"evidence of another small miracle. God answers prayer in different ways, Olivia. But whatever the answer, it's always given in love. Not judgment, not vindictiveness . . . but love. And forgiveness."

Olivia shook her head violently. "I know that! I just don't know how to accept it, internalize it . . . live it. All my life I tried to love my father; to understand him and try to forgive what he did. But nothing has worked. *Nothing*. How do you do it? How do you *know*?"

For a few moments Leya sat in thoughtful silence, absently stroking the jagged white scar on her cheek. Then she pulled one of the pins out of the simple coil holding her incredibly long hair on top of her head and held it out. "One pin at a time," she said, a look of profound sweetness flooding her face. "Life is lived one day at a time . . . just like I put this mass of hair up, one pin at a time, until it's anchored."

Seeing Olivia's gaze on her scar, she lifted her hand and lightly pressed it. "Pretty bad, isn't it? Yet it doesn't bother me at all, because for me it's a battle scar to be proud of. I received it when I was delivering a baby, many years ago, when I was only seventeen. It was also the day I met Luke." Her gaze softened into reminiscence. "He's the one who told me never to be ashamed of my less-than-perfect face, because it would remind me how I'd helped bring a new life into the world."

Olivia didn't understand, and the look of incomprehension must have been obvious.

Smiling, Cattleya tucked the pin back in place. "Luke and I had a hard time, coping with losing two babies," she explained. "Especially when one of the long-term consequences resulted in the death of a cherished dream as well. You see, Hope Hill was planned as more than just a sanctuary for abandoned or injured animals. We also wanted to turn our home into a refuge for disabled or abandoned children." Her smile was now tinged with regret. "Only my health didn't permit it."

Olivia felt the other woman's deep pain as if she had crawled inside her skin. And yet Cattleya Farringer wasn't bitter or guilt-ridden or desperate. Instead, she radiated the love of God all the way to her fingertips. "You must be helping some—Marsha, Ben—"

"We've only been able to accept foster children since last year. And when I became pregnant—and miraculously have kept this one—Luke and I engaged in several epoch-making battles. I see you find that hard to believe. Believe it, Olivia. We're blessed, and love each other very much, but we're certainly no better—or worse—than you and Jake."

"That's impossible," Olivia muttered.

"You just haven't learned to trust God like you need to," Leya finished, lumbering to her feet and moving to put on a pot of coffee. "You're a lot like Jake, you know. Both of you haven't fully grasped the truth of that wonderful eighth chapter in Romans, where Paul writes so magnificently of the nature of God's love. Remember—it's not the past that counts. It's your attitude toward the future. And since *nothing* can separate you from God's love— including and especially the past—well . . . I know that's how I . . . 'do it.' Tell you what—why don't you go check it out for yourself while I finish in here? There's a Bible in the den. The answers you find there are a lot more eloquent than mine."

"If Jake and Luke come in and find me lounging around reading while you slave in the kitchen, you'll be feeding my body parts to the birds tomorrow."

A glint appeared in Leya's dove-soft eyes. "You leave the men to me," she promised. "And, Olivia? God *wants* you to feel His love, His forgiveness, far more than you want to find it."

Forty minutes later the back door banged open and Jake burst through in a wind-and-rain-driven blast. Alerted by the sudden noise, Olivia jumped up from the couch and dashed into the kitchen. Drowsing in a chair, Leya followed more slowly.

Dripping water, Jake was hurriedly rummaging through cabinets and drawers. He looked up when they appeared, face hard, grim. "The eagle's gotten loose. We're going after it. Leya, I need flashlights, a couple of sheets, and a thermos of coffee."

Distressed, Leya didn't waste time with words. Swiftly, efficiently, she produced everything Jake required.

Olivia, standing off to the side feeling unnecessary, suddenly stepped forward. "I'll come, too. The more people you have looking, the better chance of finding him."

"No," Jake returned flatly. "It's really bad out there, Olivia. We've got half a dozen people already, and someone needs to—"

"I said I'm coming, too."

Jake raised his head and focused on Olivia for the first time. "Olivia—"

"Leya, do you have a coat I can . . . thanks." Olivia thrust her arms in the sleeves of the full-length vinyl slicker Leya grabbed from the back porch. "I'll see to the coffee while you finish finding anything else Jake wants." She shot him a brief stringent look. "Did you drive up in the Rover? Fine—I'll be waiting." And she ran out the door before he could argue with her.

"If you start whining about the weather, I'll truss you up like a goose," he threatened through clenched teeth as they jostled down the road at a bone-rattling speed. "And you'd better do exactly as you're told, or you can stay right here in this vehicle."

"Jake Donovan, you have no right to speak to me that way. I'm not some timid, hysterical little girl afraid of her own shadow. Besides, I'm good with birds. Remember Gretel?"

Lightning streaked across the sky, illuminating the harsh planes of Jake's face, the intimidating hardness of his body. He handled the Rover with ruthless skill, but the road was slick and once, when he turned sharply, Olivia fell against him with a hastily bitten off exclamation.

Incredibly, Jake chuckled. One hand left the wheel long enough to set her right. "Whatever happened to old Gretel the goose?" he asked.

"The lady licensed to take care of wild fowl came three days after Eddie ran off. I helped put Gretel in a cage, and Evie said I had an instinctive rapport that was rare and a relief for her to see."

"So there. All right, Ms. Sinclair—you've made your point."

The Rover skidded to a stop, catching in the rain-drenched yellow glow of the headlights, the silhouettes of a half-dozen or so men. Jake killed the engine, then whipped one strong arm out and hauled Olivia close. "Stay with me, and don't get lost." He lowered his head and his mouth came down on hers.

Taken off guard, Olivia stiffened. But when the bruising demand softened into warm beguiling kisses, Olivia melted in spite of herself. She forgot the storm, the eagle, the milling clutch of impatient men. Closing her eyes, she relaxed in the embrace of the man she could not stop loving any more than she could calm the storm.

Someone yanked Jake's door open. "Can't you wait until we've found the bird, Jake?" Luke growled testily. "And what'd you bring her for, anyway? Where's the stuff you were *supposed* to gather?"

Olivia jerked free, wiping her face with shaking hands. "I came to help," she offered in a pitiful attempt at dignity.

"She's got an 'instinctive rapport' with birds," Jake drawled. "Besides which, trying to stop Olivia when she's made up her mind is an exercise in futility." He tugged the hood of Olivia's slicker up and over her head, tied the strings, and dropped a last kiss on her nose. "Remember—stay with me."

Olivia clambered down from the Rover while Jake handed out the supplies. Without asking, she grabbed the coffee and styrofoam cups, filled and passed them out to the men huddled together in the entrance of the barn.

Luke appeared at her side and gratefully downed a cup of coffee in three gulps. "Sorry for what I said. I know

Leya would have been here if she could—so, thanks." In the wet, wind-blown darkness his teeth glinted briefly. "I take it you've had some experience with wild birds?"

"One Canadian goose, for three days," Jake supplied as he joined Luke, and Olivia almost yielded to the childish urge to sock his jaw. He finished handing out flashlights, then grinned at her. "But I have to admit, she did have that goose eating out of the palm of her hand."

Luke shook his head, then turned to the impatient group. "Okay, everyone. Let's get this done. He can't have gone very far but he's panicked, injured, and, therefore, dangerous. Stay with your group, and remember what I told you about working the bow net. If you find him, do not—I repeat—do *not* shout. Speak calmly, move slowly, and send someone to let me know. Now, let's go."

They split up into three groups, Olivia tagging along with Jake and two men whose size and shape were impossible to determine. Within seconds, Olivia was soaking wet in spite of the protective covering, her face streaming water, vision blurred. She must have been insane to think she could help.

"He can't fly," Jake spoke right next to her ear, "except in short six- or seven-foot hops. So look in the underbrush, and in lower limbs." He thrust a pencil-thin Swiss Army flashlight into her hand. "Here. Try not to shine that in your face or anyone else's. It will take a while for your night vision to kick in, but do the best you can."

"I will."

Shivering and drenched, half-blind, Olivia tried to creep through the sodden undergrowth quietly, though the stinging sheets of rain and rumbling thunder masked the noise of everyone's movement. Wiping her eyes constantly, she moved the light in a steady back-and-forth motion, strain-ing to see. Praying they would find the bird in time.

Scant feet away, she sensed Jake's presence, occasion-ally caught the rustling sound of his clothing. She obediently avoided the sweeping light of his high-beam flashlight, and she refused to dwell on either her sodden misery or the anguished look she'd glimpsed on Luke Farringer's face. Back and forth swept her little circle of light as she stumbled along, branches smacking her face and clawing at Leya's slicker. The light passed over a dark mass low in the swaying branches of some kind of hardwood tree.

Olivia took two more steps, then froze. "Jake," she hissed urgently. Turning, she carefully trained her light on the dark mass. It moved! Olivia dropped the beam and sidestepped through a spongy patch of underbrush, hand flailing out to snag a wet fold of Jake's heavy waterproof leather parka.

He stopped. "What is it?"

"Over there, in that tree . . . a little up and to the right of my beam." Her voice trembled with excitement, and she felt Jake's hand briefly press her shoulder.

"I see it. Way to go, sweetheart. That's our bird!" He melted away to alert the other two men.

Seconds later, heart pounding, Olivia followed the trio at a distance, clutching several flashlights so the men could better work their bow net. Six feet from their quarry, they paused. The eagle roused and tried to flee. Only one wing unfurled, causing the majestic bird to tumble grace-lessly toward the ground, huge yellow feet clawing wildly at the earth.

Moving with blinding speed, Jake darted around the

other side of the tree while the two men approached from the front. Lifting the net high, spreading it wide, they swooped down upon the struggling creature and dropped the mesh over its head. Jake pulled the cord—and it was over.

Olivia didn't realize that the wetness on her face was not only rain, but tears, until her nose plugged up. Moving as calmly as she could, she joined Jake by the bird's side while one of the men took off to alert Luke.

"Don't come too close," Jake warned. "Luke has the rufter and jesses, and until he gets here, keep your distance. One of the bird's talons is pretty weak, but it's still lethal."

"It's awful, having to restrain him like this." Oblivious to prickly clinging leaves and soggy earth, Olivia sank to her knees, eyes never leaving the bound and helpless bird. "It's okay," she began to murmur, as if she were talking to Gretel. "Don't worry—we aren't going to hurt you. We want to help you—so you're free again. Free to soar high, be the majestic bird God designed you to be—" Tears crowded her throat, but she kept talking, kept crooning a hoarse meaningless torrent of words.

And the eagle watched her, dark eye unblinking, gray beak quiescent.

Ten minutes later Luke arrived with the leather thongs and hood. Working with incredible speed and gentleness, in a short while he freed the now blind and snaffled bird from the confining net. With almost magical skill, he coaxed the eagle onto his forearm, over the heavy gauntlet, and began the long careful walk back through the woods.

Standing back out of the way, Olivia watched, heart overflowing. When Jake came to tell her it was time to go, all she could do was stare mutely up through the pouring rain into his blurred face. She couldn't see his expression, but all of a sudden his hands were cupping her face. Cold and wet, his touch was warm, and Olivia closed her eyes. He kissed her eyelids, her forehead.

"It's okay," he soothed as Olivia had tried to calm the eagle, his words low, laced with tenderness. "He'll be all right now. And you were great . . . wouldn't be surprised if Luke offered you a job. Shh, now . . . don't cry." He wiped clinging strands of hair away.

Giggling wetly, Olivia rested her cheek against the clammy front of Jake's parka. "I don't know what's the matter with me." She sighed. "Here we are in the woods, in a crash-bang thunderstorm in the middle of the night, and all I can do is weep. It's just . . . the eagle. To be so helpless and humiliated like that, and we were just trying to help—" Her voice broke again. "Jake—"

He hugged her, wet slicker and all, then grabbed her hand. "Come on, let's get back to warmth and light, and then we'll talk." His hand tightened, then relaxed. "And this time," Olivia thought she heard him say, "this time, we're going to settle things once and for all."

# eighteen

As if to atone for the fury of the storm, the sun rose from behind the hills the next morning, draping the land in a warm shimmering veil of rosy light. Leaves dripped prism-colored droplets, and steam rose in a pearly mist among the gleaming wet tree trunks. By eight, the sky burned an enamel-bright blue, as clear and clean as the twins' innocent eyes.

Jake watched, trying to hide his amusement, while Luke corralled his sons and herded them into the Rover. Since Leya had her weekly check-up with the obstetrician today, Luke planned to drop all the kids off at the county school on the way down. On the way home after lunch, they'd pick Josh and Joey up at kindergarten.

"This is your chance, my friend," Luke told Jake. "For several hours there should be peace and quiet around here, so you and Olivia can sort out your respective snarls . . . spiritual and physical." He hesitated, a quizzical gleam shading the blue eyes. "If you'd like a little well-intended advice—try to keep your hands to yourself. I almost blew it once upon a time, because the flesh is particularly weak when you're dealing with the woman you love."

Leya came up then, slipping her arm about her husband's waist and lifting her face for his kiss. "We both know how easy it is, when you're young," she added, watching Jake out of those serene, dovelike eyes of hers.

Just then Joshua came flying off the front steps to land

162

with a satisfying splash in a puddle, propelling muddy water all over his brother's clean shirt and slacks.

"That's it," snarled Luke, hauling both boys up and tucking one under each arm. "Cattleya!" he roared. "Let's get going before I have to tie these little rug rats to the bumper!" He winked at Jake. "They love it when I talk tough."

Leya strolled out on the porch, behind Marsha and Ben. She was listening to Olivia, who was promising to make sure the kitchen was cleaned, the beds made . . . and would Leya hush her fretting. Olivia could handle things just fine. Then her gaze met Jake's, and she turned as fiery pink as the row of azaleas blazing on either side of the porch steps.

Leya waved, then turned to hug Olivia. "Don't forget," she told her.

Moments later, with a last farewell toot of the horn, the Rover disappeared around the curve, and silence descended with a thud.

Jake began walking toward Olivia. "Don't forget what?" he asked, watching her step back, looking as shy and skittish as one of Luke's mustang fillies. He stopped, propping his hip on the porch rail and stuffing his hands in his waistband.

"I'd rather . . . not say just yet," Olivia replied. "I—um—I need to go clean the kitchen. I promised Leya and—"

"Come here, sweetheart." He didn't move, though inside he was melting with laughter and love. Olivia's hesitancy was almost comical. Never in his life had he met a woman of such contrasts—one moment radiating the calm authority of a general; the next, the entrancing uncertainty of a school girl, oblivious to her own charms. *Dear God, I love this woman. Help me here, okay? And oh, yes—give me the strength to resist the very powerful temptation. . . .*

She paused three feet away, hovering, blue-gray eyes wide, unblinking as a fawn's. "Why are you looking at me like that?"

"Like what?"

Olivia shrugged, her nose wrinkling. "Like you're trying to decide where to bite first."

He straightened and took a step, forcing her with the power of his will not to retreat, his gaze burning steadily, watching her pupils expand until they all but drowned out the irises. "Olivia . . . I've got something to tell you. You know that, don't you?"

She was shaking her head, hands coming up to fend him off. "I—I don't want to hear it," she stammered. "Jake—it's impossible, whatever it is."

"Don't you know, my darling, that with God, *all* things are possible? Even you and me?" He lifted his hand, wiping away a single tear with the pad of his thumb. "*Especially* you and me. Olivia, I love you . . . and I know you love me." Taking her hands between his, he kissed her, a brief but tender caress. "And—because I feel your fear all the way to the soles of my feet—I want you to know I also accepted Jesus as my Lord and Savior. Weeks ago, in point of fact. Not just because I love you and knew that would be the only way I could have you . . . but because *He* loves *me*."

Olivia still didn't speak, just stood there looking at him in drowning misery. Jake was suddenly very uneasy. He'd bared his heart, leaving himself wide open and totally vulnerable. If she turned away from him now, he'd never recover. "Remember last night," he questioned desperately, urgently, "when we trapped the eagle? Remember how you felt?"

Slowly she nodded.

"You wanted that bird to understand that we weren't going to hurt it, or keep it caged. That we just wanted to help, so it would be free to soar like God intended?"

Throat muscles working, Olivia nodded again. "I remember," she whispered.

"That's what God does for us." Jake crammed his hands back in his jeans. "It's taken me weeks—years!—but I understand now who God really is. He wants to do for us what Luke will do for that eagle. He wants to free us to soar, carried by His love. *Love* . . . not judgment, Olivia. That's what being a Christian means. It's not all the thou-shalt-nots and the thou-musts. It's not the angry God with the big stick Aunt Sophy used to threaten me with. It's Jesus, dying on a cross because He loved us.

"Luke showed me a verse last week, where Jesus Himself says He came not to judge, but to save. Olivia, judgment is reserved only for those who reject Him, *not* for those of us struggling to follow Him. That's the miracle of it all. He gives us love and forgiveness, not seven times or seventy times . . . *every* time." He paused to watch her carefully, his voice very soft, very gentle. "Olivia . . . you have to believe it. You have to believe *me*. I love you . . . God loves you."

Unable to control himself any longer, he hauled her into his arms and held her close, pressing her head against his heart, the words spewing forth uncontrollably. "Let the past go—let your father go. You have to forgive, Olivia. That's all. You don't have to work for it, you can't earn it . . . and the burden is not yours to carry. Give it to God."

"I tried. I *can't*." She wrenched free, facing him with the angry passion of total desperation. "I don't know *how* to forgive—and because I can't, God won't forgive *me*. The Bible says that, too. Jesus even told a story about it— the one with the servant who ends up in jail because he wouldn't forgive his fellow servant's debt? That's me. I'm in jail, and I know it. And I can't get out." White-faced and pleading, she searched Jake's face. "Jake—"

Frustrated, Jake gripped the back of a wooden rocking chair. She wasn't listening, and he couldn't *make* her understand. "You're a Christian," he grated, fear driving his words like the crack of a whip. "That means at some point in the last twenty years or so, you had to accept—in your heart—that Jesus Christ paid for every sin you ever committed, past, present, and future, right? You accepted it, didn't you? You didn't earn it, or work for it, or beg for it!" Olivia jerked under the lash of his tongue, but Jake was too angry now to care.

Control rapidly eroded as all the old instincts crowded back. "If you can accept the fact that God forgives you for all those unnamed sins, why in the name of common sense, can't you also give Him the burden of your father? If you really loved me, Olivia, you'd at least make the effort!"

The moment the words left his mouth, he regretted them, but it was too late. Olivia's face turned the color of dirty laundry, and her dilated eyes began to lose focus. Moving stiffly, she crept toward the railing, leaning against it as if she'd fall down without its support.

"I didn't mean that, Olivia. I—" Jake clamped his mouth shut. His feelings were boiling, his newfound faith in tatters. Thanks to his blasted temper, he'd just sent the woman he loved spiraling into another catatonic trance to escape his vicious tongue. *I'm no better than her old man, Lord.*

Filled with self-hatred, his eyes swept over a frozen Olivia. "Don't worry," he bit out, "I'm hanging it up. When the Farringers get back, tell them I'd appreciate it if they'd see about your return to North Carolina. I'll be in touch." He stalked past Olivia into the house, slamming the door.

Two hours later, loaded down with his gear, he left. Tromping across the meadow with the sun shining on his head and the soft spring wind filling the air, Jake was conscious only of Olivia as he'd left her—eyes glazed in a face drained of all color and expression. The way he'd botched things, he'd probably killed her love as well.

As the shadows lengthened, Jake faced some of the most painful realizations of his new life as a Christian—old habits die hard, and every love story doesn't end happily ever after.

# nineteen

Olivia drove to Sherm's Shelter the evening after her return to North Carolina. At home, silence screamed at her; at work, Maria and Rollie fretted and petted and worried her to death. She couldn't call her mother because it would only upset her, and the last person she wanted to talk to was Beth.

So she drove to Sherm's. There she could be with people whose needs were far more fundamental than Olivia's fractured heart. And, to her great relief, Sherm stayed too busy to pick her brain about Jake.

Even the thought of him made her hands cold and clammy, and sickness still swam in her veins when she remembered their parting. He hadn't even said goodbye.

She parked under the brightest light in the parking lot. Sergeant MacClary's lead had proven to be another dead end, so Olivia continued to be extra careful. Sometimes, though, she was tempted to stake herself out like a tethered goat and get it over with.

"Evening, O-LIV-i-a," Sherm called from across the room, where he was sweeping the floor. "Missed you last week, gal."

"I missed being here, too." Olivia did her best to inject some life into her voice. She smiled at the greetings of various regulars as she walked over. "What needs doing this evening?"

"Well . . . seeing as how you've been gone a spell, I guess

for starters, maybe you'd better apologize to everyone. We've missed your smiling—hey!" he broke off. "What's this?" Sherm quit sweeping and peered down into Olivia's hastily averted face. "Don't tell me you're crying."

He sounded so appalled that a tiny spark of laughter helped to stave off the aching tears. When she recovered from all this—if she ever did—Olivia vowed she would never cry again as long as she lived. It was a debasing, useless, humiliating emotion, just like her father used to say.

"Sorry," she eventually managed, with a fair amount of control. "Something must have flown into my eye— probably a speck of dust." She shook off his concern. "Looks like you're through with dinner. How 'bout if I fetch my box of goodies from the trunk of my car. We did a wedding over the weekend, and they had so much food left from the reception, they practically *begged* me to take it off their hands. I thought of you, and—here we are."

Sherm shook his balding, pony-tailed head. "If that don't beat the berries. You're all right, Ms. O-LIV-i-a Sinclair. Need any help?"

"I can handle it. Go on with your sweeping."

She unloaded one box and returned for the last one. As she passed the end of the building just before reaching the parking lot, she glimpsed a sudden movement from the corner of her eye. Alarm kicked through Olivia. She took one step backward, preparing to run, or scream . . . or both.

"Psst. 'Livia! It's me—Eddie!"

Mouth cotton-dry, Olivia hesitated, still poised to flee. "Eddie?"

A shuffling, hesitant shadow separated itself from the wall, and Eddie sidled into the corner of the security lights.

"Been waitin' here, every evenin' for you." He cleared his throat and spat, scuffing a battered loafer in the dirt. "Wanted to say I was sorry. You was nice to me and Nan . . . Nan, that's what I named her, y'know. I found out what happened, how she went to a place where they'll take care of her wing so's she can fly."

"Thank you for coming back." Light-headed with relief, Olivia was nonetheless touched and humbled by this poor wretched man's honesty. She had to make him understand that it was okay. "I know you didn't mean anything. You were just scared, just wanted to protect . . . Nan."

"Nan's my wife's name. She died four years, seven months, twenty-one days ago." He blinked at Olivia, the sad, sunken old eyes almost childlike. "I miss her. Don't see much use in livin' without her, so I just sort of amble around, waitin' to die. It felt real good to help that old bird, though."

"I know," Olivia said softly. "Eddie, why don't you come inside with me now? I've got a lot of delicious food, and—"

"No. Don't want no more trouble. Just had to wait until I could tell you thanks." He shifted uneasily, looking furtively around. "And—and it weren't me that slashed your tires, 'Livia—"

"Oh, Eddie, I knew that."

"—but I did see who done it, and that's the other reason I been watchin' here, waitin' every night." He cleared his throat, spat again. "She's here, 'Livia . . . and I had to tell you, so's you can be careful."

Olivia felt as if she were seeing Eddie through the wrong end of a telescope. "She's *here*?" She forced the words past constricted throat muscles. "The . . . woman . . . who slashed my tires?" Dazed, blood roaring in her ears, she wondered, with some remnant of lucidity, what Eddie would do if she nose-dived right at his feet. *If it's the same woman, then it must be the stalker. The one who vandalized the house. Threw a brick at me.*

" 'Livia? I had to tell you, didn't I? But I don't want no trouble, so I gotta go." He reached beneath the same filthy jacket he'd been wearing weeks ago and pulled out a newspaper-wrapped bundle, thrusting it toward Olivia. "And—and I wanted to give this back. I—it's too fine for me. It would be a . . . I mean, it would do my heart good if you'd take it back." The paper unfurled and a fold of lavender knit spilled out.

As if in a dream, Olivia accepted her sweater.

"I'm gonna take off now—you be careful, y'hear? That old woman . . . she's been here every night, just like me. It's like she's waitin', too."

Olivia closed her eyes. "I . . . see. Thank you, Eddie. You've been a big help. And—I'll always think of you when I wear this sweater."

He ducked his head, then turned. "Eddie!" She darted after him, touching the bony shoulder. "Eddie, that woman? Where is she?"

Hunching down, he peeked around Olivia, lifting his arm and pointing a trembling finger. "Right yonder, 'cross the street by them dumpsters. She parks there, outta sight. She don't even notice me—" He shifted nervously. "You'll be careful?"

Olivia patted his shoulder. "I'll be very careful, Eddie. Are you sure you won't come inside?"

But Eddie had already melted back into the night, a lonely, forgotten old man who quite possibly had just saved Olivia's life. Moving stiffly on legs which had no feeling, she headed back toward the common room.

Sherm called the police, explained the situation, and stashed Olivia in a corner of the kitchen. There she sat, fidgeting and anxious, while Sherm peeled potatoes and rattled off old football stories to distract her while she waited.

But it was a good thirty minutes before a wiry patrolman sauntered into the room and Sherm went to meet him, motioning for Olivia to stay put. Ignoring him, she rose and followed.

"Olivia Sinclair?"

"Yes. Did you—*was* there a woman behind the dumpster?"

"Yes, ma'am. Ma'am?" the police officer asked abruptly. "Do you need to sit down?"

And the next thing Olivia knew, Sherm had snagged a chair and shoved her into it as if she were a sack of meal.

"I'm fine," she insisted, shaking her head to clear the ringing. Smiling a little, she amended, "Well, almost. May I see her please, Officer?" Looking stern, the policeman was about to refuse. But Olivia insisted. "I'd really like to see this woman. I don't plan to make a scene or do anything foolish . . . but I need to see her. She's outside?"

Without waiting for a response, she headed across the room, having found long ago that sometimes more was accomplished by charging full steam ahead while asking permission to do so. The disgruntled cop caught up with her at the door and escorted her to a squad car, where a female detective was trying in vain to stem the vituperative flow of words gushing from the mouth of a dainty little old woman, barely five feet tall.

When she caught sight of Olivia, the woman screeched and would have lunged at her, except for the restraining handcuffs joining her to the long-suffering detective. "You deserved it! All of it! You have no right to walk around free when my daughter's life is ruined! Ruined!"

"That's enough," snapped the detective, but Olivia calmly faced the infuriated woman.

"It was my father, wasn't it, who ruined your daughter?" she clarified.

"Yes!" shouted the woman, shaking her free fist. "Yes, your father, Alton almighty Sinclair, may he burn forever!"

With a warning look, the patrolman moved to stand at her side. "This is not a good idea, Ms. Sinclair," the detective said. "We've read her her rights, and she claims to understand. Nevertheless, this is highly irregular, especially since your presence is only inciting her further."

"I don't care," the woman hissed, practically vibrating with the force of her emotion. "All these years, watching my Alice, knowing what that no-good, sorry—" She stopped, slanting a sly look to either side before shooting Olivia a triumphant, malevolent glare. "I couldn't do anything to your father, but I waited. And then you came, begging my daughter to forgive. *Forgive!*" She spat the word as if it were an obscenity. "She spent three years in therapy, and lost her job, her husband—everything! And nobody knew what your father did except me. Sometimes I thought Alice would take her own life. Do you know what that does to a mother? Do you have any idea what I've been through?" All of a sudden the seething anger dissipated. With a dry, heaving sob, the woman began to cry.

Reeling with shocked recognition, Olivia heard the familiar words as though she herself were speaking. She understood that kind of pain, even understood why she was the target of the woman's venom. This hurting mother had simply attacked the only available substitute for Alton Sinclair himself.

"What's her name?" Olivia asked the detective.

"Sylvia Blecker, Hickory address. You ever see this woman before?"

An errant memory flickered, then crystallized. "In Statesville," Olivia said slowly, staring hard at the defeated old woman with her gray hair fashioned in tight permed ringlets. "It was you that day, wasn't it. . . . You ran the light on purpose, tried to run me down?"

"If that boy hadn't pulled you back, it all would have been over," Mrs. Blecker muttered dully. "It would have been over, and I'd be free. You'd have paid for what your father did to my daughter."

You'd have paid. . . . *This is my body, broken for you. He who did not spare His own Son, but gave Him for us all.* . . .

Olivia felt as if the sun had just hurtled from the sky into her chest, exploding in a blinding, burning fireball of spiritual illumination. As if she were walking along the road to Damascus instead of Paul, Olivia felt her entire life change in one revelatory instant. *Felt* the change in her head, in her heart.

Lifting wondering eyes to the suddenly silent trio of faces watching her, Olivia finally knew with absolute clarity what she had to do. And along with that knowledge flowed a single rivulet of peace, calm and serenely blue as a summer sky at twilight.

Olivia stepped right up to Mrs. Blecker, so close she could see the sweat beading her upper lip. Looked into the tearful, bloodshot eyes and saw the bottomless pit of vengeance slowly destroying Sylvia Blecker's soul. "Mrs. Blecker, we both must accept the fact that nothing I say or do can change what my father did to your daughter. Can you do that?" she asked, very gently.

Mouth working, blinking rapidly, the older woman stared down at her feet for what seemed like an eternity. Then she nodded, once, not looking at Olivia.

Olivia felt as if she were floating in a cloud high above the misery and drama of the ravaged earth. "And would you be willing to accept, here and now, that there is nothing *you* can do—including hurting me—that will *undo* what my father did to your daughter?"

The two policemen stirred restlessly, but Olivia reassured them with eloquent eyes, so confident of her decision that the certainty pulsed from her heart all the way to her fingertips. Shrugging, the female detective nodded in agreement.

With great effort Sylvia Blecker lifted her head to search Olivia's face. "I—it hasn't helped," the syllables dragged out. "I thought if I could watch you suffer, do something to you that would make you hurt like my daughter was hurt, that I'd feel better."

"Why haven't you done something to my store? You've been following me, you know where it is. Why?"

Looking old and shrunken, gaze dropping to the hard metal handcuff enclosing her wrist, Mrs. Blecker mumbled, half-sheepishly, "I wanted to hurt you, not anyone else. I saw all those young people coming and going, all of them leaving with smiles on their faces. So glowing, so full of life like my Alice used to be." Her mouth trembled as tears oozed from the corner of her eyelids again. "I didn't want to hurt anybody else." She slumped back against the patrol car. "And . . . and I guess I sort of realized, deep down, that you weren't anything like your father. Only by then I just couldn't let it go. All that anger . . . like a hard knot deep inside, and all I could do was just keep on."

Olivia inhaled slowly. "Mrs. Blecker," she said, each word falling into a silence so intense it seemed even the crickets were holding their breath, "would it help that knot to go away if I promised you that I truly understand why you did all those things, and that I—that I forgive you?"

Mrs. Blecker's chin quivered, and the tears ran faster. "I was wrong, I'll have to pay—I'll have to go to prison—"

There was a long pause before Olivia spoke again. "Not if I refuse to press charges."

The woman gasped, and one of the officers stepped forward to protest. "Ms. Sinclair, this discussion needs to take place in the presence of a lawyer. You can't make that kind of decision based on the emotion of the moment."

Olivia picked up Mrs. Blecker's thin hand and gave it a gentle squeeze. "It's not a fleeting emotion," she promised quietly. "Mrs. Blecker, you have to let go of what my father did. It's in the past. Don't let his wickedness destroy your life, too. Trust me . . . I understand."

"But how can you possibly forgive what I did to you—your house—your car?" She jerked her hand free and covered her eyes, weeping.

The tranquil blue stream flooding Olivia's heart widened into an ocean of love. "How can I?" she repeated in a voice bubbling with light, effervescent joy. "Actually . . . it's incredibly easy, easier than I could have ever imagined." She shook her head, as if not quite believing it herself. "Mrs. Blecker," she began again, "from the bottom of my heart, I do forgive you. Now, how about coming back inside with me? We'll share some leftover wedding goodies, and you can tell me about your daughter."

Looking disgusted and disillusioned, the detective unlocked the handcuffs. "I think you're making a big mistake," she informed Olivia with rigid formality.

"Thank you for coming so promptly, Officers." Smiling, Olivia put her arm around the stunned, unresisting Mrs. Blecker. "You won't believe this, I know, but everything really *is* going to be fine."

Shaking their heads, the two climbed into their car and sped off, while Olivia led a trembling, hopeful Sylvia Blecker toward the warmth and welcoming light of Sherm's Shelter. She couldn't wait to tell Maria and Rollie that the stalker had been caught, and that she'd invited her in for tea.

And someday—*soon, Lord*?—she'd be able to tell Jake she was out of her own prison, on permanent parole.

# twenty

Wandering around the Chattahoochee National Forest like John the Baptist in the wilderness didn't help.

Another exhilarating, challenging run down the Chattooga rapids fell flat.

Landing back on the Farringers' doorstep hungry, dirty, and exhausted earned him food, bed, and a bath—and some comforting words. But no peace.

More unsure of himself than he'd ever been in his entire life, Jake at last flew back to North Carolina, where his only hope for reconciliation and joy rested in the fragile heart of the woman whose spirit his blasted temper had crushed. Maybe permanently. A Christian woman who'd never learned how to forgive.

He delayed long enough in Charlotte to buy the only Range Rover sitting on the lot—a black one that suited his present mood. Ignoring the salesman's flabbergasted sputterings, Jake signed papers, slapped down a personal check that left everyone gasping at the ease with which it cleared, and took himself and his new vehicle off.

Driving with grim determination up I-77 toward Barley, Jake spared scant seconds to enjoy the first automobile he'd owned in almost a decade. Instead, he spent the entire journey playing and replaying in his mind all the potential scenarios with Olivia which could unfold. At the far end of the spectrum, he nursed a growing fear that she would end up in the room next to Davy, her mind forever imprisoned in mental as well as spiritual chains.

When he almost missed his exit onto the state road, Jake punched in a cassette tape of Christian music Tony, his old teammate, had given him. Jake still preferred his golden oldies. But right now he needed spiritual nurturing more than entertainment.

Naturally, it was a gray, dingy afternoon, the air muggy and rife with noxious odors produced by civilization. *Well, Donovan,* he thought with wry humor, *the mood you're in, she's sure to jump right into your arms and welcome you home.*

His chest felt like a hot poker was probing around. And when a sign indicating a roadside picnic area flashed by, Jake hit the brakes. Pulling up under a stand of loblolly pines, he switched off the engine, leaned back against the new-smelling leather seat, and closed his eyes.

*This is it, God. Luke claims You really do know when we're at the end of our rope, and all You require is that we let go and fall into Your waiting arms. Well . . . I gave up last week, and if You don't catch me, I'm afraid the fall this time might be fatal. I don't deserve Your forgiveness, much less Olivia's . . . but I guess I either accept those words I hurled at her in anger—or choke on them.*

Jake opened his eyes, feeling a totally foreign stinging sensation at the corners. Lifting a wondering hand, he swiped at the salty drops; for the first time in over thirty years, he was actually crying. *Father, forgive me. Then help us both.* He restarted the engine, then paused, a sheepish grin hovering at the corners of his mouth. Aloud, he finished the heartfelt prayer, "And, God . . . thanks."

Only one car was parked in front of The Bridal Bower. As Jake pulled in two spots down, the door opened and two women emerged, heading for the car. *So far, so good,* he thought, waiting until the women headed off down the street. Then he climbed out, took a deep breath, and entered the lion's den.

Of course, when a man has primed himself for battle, but the bugler plays "Here Comes the Bride," most of the drama is reduced to farce. A lopsided grin, unwanted but relentless, spread across Jake's face when Maria glanced up to see who had come through the door.

Her brown eyes opened wide, then narrowed, and she rushed over to meet him. But instead of the tongue-lashing Jake expected and deserved, Maria grabbed his arm and hauled him toward the back room.

"It's about time," she hissed out of the corner of her mouth. "We've been on pins and needles and thumbtacks, waiting for you to finally stick your gorgeous body but stubborn head through the door." She whipped her head around to make sure the room was empty. "This is great! We don't have any appointments scheduled until three-thirty." She surveyed Jake archly. "You *are* here as the handsome prince instead of the wicked villain, aren't you?"

Jake finally found his wits. He felt light-headed, as if he'd inhaled a tankful of nitrous oxide. "Olivia?" For some reason he couldn't manage anything more, but every hope, every longing, and every bit of love he had for her was invested in that one word.

Maria reached up and kissed his cheek. "She's here, and she's fine. And she needs you as much as you need her, Jake. Go on . . . it's all right." She gave him a push, then flashed a saucy grin. "Trust me."

Moving like a sleepwalker, Jake made his way down the aisle, around a dressmaker's form clad in a wedding gown, and to the door of Olivia's office. When he put out his hand to open it, he saw that his fingers were actually shaking.

Olivia and Rollie were at Rollie's desk, talking. They both looked up when Jake came into the room, but Jake hadn't a clue as to Rollie's response. He was looking at the woman he loved . . . and he couldn't tear his gaze away.

She didn't look like the same Olivia. Blue sparkles of joy crowded out the gray of her eyes. And when she spoke, she sounded as if she'd inhaled a thousand sunbeams.

"Jake—" She mouthed his name, then shouted it joyously, "Jake!" Slowly straightening, she moved out from behind the desk, and took one dreamlike step toward him.

Suddenly the words bubbled forth, as swift and free as the Farringers' creek after a rain. "Olivia, I'm sorry. I'm an insensitive, selfish, hot-headed louse and I don't deserve anything after the way I treated you. But I love you and I want to marry you . . . mmph!"

Olivia hurled herself into his arms, hugging him so tight he couldn't have pried her loose with a crowbar. "I love *you*, and I'm sorry, too, and—and you were right and I was wrong!"

This time Jake interrupted Olivia, but only with his mouth, kissing her with all the pent-up longing of the past week of self-reproach and fear. He kissed her soft, trembling lips, her eyes, her cheeks, the pulse throbbing in her temple, all the while trying to whisper his love, his shame, his need for her to understand. To forgive.

Olivia somehow managed to wriggle her hand between

them and gently lay it over his mouth. "I have so much to tell you," she said, her eyes shining with love and peace.

"As long as it's yes, I don't care what else you have to say," he murmured. But even so, Jake held his breath.

"Later." She laughed. "I have a few things that have to come first . . . like, I forgive you—from deep down in my heart—so you can stop hating yourself for what happened at the Farringers'."

His hands gripped her shoulders urgently. Then, with exquisite tenderness, he tilted her chin up with his thumbs. "What's happened, sweetheart?"

"Just like I said . . . you were right and I was wrong," Olivia repeated, gazing up at him with her heart in her eyes. "Jake, I've learned more about being a Christian in the past week than I have since I accepted Jesus as my Savior twenty years ago."

"And what's that?" He lovingly caressed the blush heating her cheeks. "And what was it I was so 'right' about?"

"Forgiveness. You can't earn it, or work for it." She closed her eyes briefly, and when the translucent lids lifted, a sheen of tears shimmered like sunlight off the surface of a lake. "It's your attitude—and you can't *force* your attitude to change. You can only accept God's promise to *help* you change. And . . . and it just happens. In your head, in your heart. Like a beautiful sunrise. Like Easter morning. It's *real*, Jake."

He brought his forehead down to rest against hers, so weak with relief, with gratitude he didn't know how he was still standing. "I love you."

From behind them Rollie finally spoke up, her voice testy but indulgent. "Not that my presence has put a damper on your latest, and hopefully *last*, reunion . . . but if you can break it up long enough for Olivia to tell you the news about the stalker, I'll give you some privacy."

Jake turned to face her, still holding Olivia. "What about the stalker?"

Looking like a plump broody hen, rocking back in her desk chair and watching unabashedly, Rollie heaved herself to her feet and chuckled. "I'm dying to see your face when she explains. Go on, Olivia—tell the man."

Flushed and laughing, Olivia tugged at Jake's hands, and he reluctantly released her. "You're incorrigible," Olivia informed her partner, "and I think maybe I should fire you."

"Fire away," Rollie retorted.

Throwing up her hands, Olivia took a couple of steps back and clasped her hands. "I don't know what you're going to think of this, Jake," she confessed a little bit nervously.

Jake's eyebrow lifted. "Right now I'm thinking if you don't get on with it, Rollie's going to be very disappointed, because in two seconds I plan to show her the door myself." Then, when Olivia continued to stand there chewing her lip, he pressed, more gently, "Just tell me. What's happened with the stalker? Has she finally been apprehended, I hope?"

"Yes . . . in a manner of speaking."

Maria slipped through the door to add her two cents. "What Olivia is hesitant to share is that, after catching the woman in the act, hearing her confess to everything—*and* with the police standing there holding the woman in handcuffs—Olivia refused to press charges."

High as the heavens within the security of their restored

relationship, Jake merely cast Olivia a questioning look. "And why would she do that?" he drawled, drawing his finger down the cheek that a month ago had been an ugly, swollen mess.

"I had to, Jake. You see—that's when I finally understood about forgiveness. Her name's Sylvia Blecker, and six years ago her daughter was one of my father's victims . . . one of the people who slammed the door in my face when I tried to talk with her. Her mother—Mrs. Blecker—happened to be there that day, and when I left, she followed me."

"And set out to get revenge." He winced, thinking of his own unholy agenda.

"Jake, she was hurting just like me, and if I hadn't dropped the charges, she could have gone to jail for aggravated assault. The only way out . . . for *both* of us was for me to forgive her—" A single tear slid down her cheek. "So, you see, I had to do it. I—I—"

"It's okay, sweetheart. I understand." He tugged her back into his arms. "Only moments ago I felt like I was behind bars myself . . . and until you forgave me, there was no way out for me either."

Relief sagged her shoulders. "You *do* understand, don't you?" she breathed. "Now we're free."

"As an eagle." Jake winked.

"As a forgiven child of God," Olivia amended. "Remember that parable? The one that always bothered me because the servant was thrown in jail until he paid his debt?"

"I remember."

"I understand what Jesus was trying to teach now. The master wasn't worried about the money owed—he just wanted the servant's attitude, his *heart* to change. You know what else? I'll bet that jail wasn't even locked, because the servant had put himself there and slammed the cell door shut. Just like I did . . . like Mrs. Blecker—"

Jake hugged her close. "And then you got smart, didn't you, and finally heard what God had been trying to tell you all the time? That He sent Jesus to cancel your debt, mark your account 'Paid in Full,' and set you free once and for all. And that it's a pretty heartless businesswoman who wouldn't pass that kind of deal along to the next person."

"Enough sermonizing already," Maria piped up. "When's the wedding?"

Jake and Olivia gaped open-mouthed at Maria, then at each other. Then he watched the blue-gray eyes transform back to teasing blue.

"Statistically speaking," Olivia began, "couples who have known each other less than a year should have longer engagements."

"Oh, no you don't, Ms. Sinclair! No more delays." Jake planted a lusty kiss right on her lips. "Say yes, or I'll have to resort to more drastic forms of persuasion."

"Yes!" Olivia cried. "But, Jake," she whispered, sobering, "I can't promise that longstanding behavior patterns will disappear instantly. I have to be honest— you've seen what I allowed my father's warped character to do to me."

Jake held her at arm's length. "You've seen that I still have a lousy temper," he intoned solemnly.

"And *I* still have a daily planner."

"This is getting serious. I might even have to give in to the urge to take off for the wilderness every now and then."

"*I* might give in to the urge to come along. I could

organize the trips, coordinate times——" She twisted out of his arms, laughing.

Jake charged. Squealing, Olivia darted behind a table. Rollie and Maria prudently edged toward the door, while Jake stalked his quarry. She feinted left.

Jake followed suit, catching her easily, and wagging his finger. "*Never* try to outmaneuver an ex-pro wide receiver."

In a quick economy of motion that left Olivia breathless, he whisked her off her feet and carried her over to Rollie and Maria. "The three of you can plan the wedding," he announced, "but *I'll* take care of the honeymoon." Lowering his head, he captured the lips of his bride-to-be in another long, thoroughly satisfying kiss. *On the other hand, I think I'll leave the happy ending to You, Lord. . . .*

Unnoticed, Rollie and Maria slipped out, closing the door behind them. "Well," Maria said, sighing, "at least they've come to the best place in three counties to plan a wedding. Come on, Rollie. Let's get busy."

# *A Letter To Our Readers*

Dear Reader:

In order that we might better contribute to your reading enjoyment, we would appreciate your taking a few minutes to respond to the following questions. When completed, please return to the following:

Karen Carroll, Editor
Heartsong Presents
P.O. Box 719
Uhrichsville, Ohio 44683

1. Did you enjoy reading *From the Heart?*
   ☐ Very much. I would like to see more books by this author!
   ☐ Moderately
   I would have enjoyed it more if _____

   _____

2. Are you a member of *Heartsong Presents*?   Yes   No
   If no, where did you purchase this book? _____

   _____

3. What influenced your decision to purchase this book? (Circle those that apply.)

   Cover              Back cover copy

   Title              Friends

   Publicity          Other _____

4. On a scale from 1 (poor) to 10 (superior), please rate the following elements.

___Heroine     ___Plot

___Hero     ___Inspirational theme

___Setting     ___Secondary characters

5. What settings would you like to see covered in *Heartsong Presents* books?

_____

_____

6. What are some inspirational themes you would like to see treated in future books?_____

_____

_____

7. Would you be interested in reading other *Heartsong Presents* titles?     Yes     No

8. Please circle your age range:

| | | |
|---|---|---|
| Under 18 | 18-24 | 25-34 |
| 35-45 | 46-55 | Over 55 |

9. How many hours per week do you read? _____

Name _____

Occupation _____

Address _____

City _____ State _____ Zip _____

# LOVE A GREAT LOVE STORY?

*Introducing Heartsong Presents —*
*Your Inspirational Book Club*

Heartsong Presents Christian romance reader's service will provide you with four never before published romance titles every month! In fact, your books will be mailed to you at the same time advance copies are sent to book reviewers. You'll preview each of these new and unabridged books before they are released to the general public.

These books are filled with the kind of stories you have been longing for—stories of courtship, chivalry, honor, and virtue. Strong characters and riveting plot lines will make you want to read on and on. Romance is not dead, and each of these romantic tales will remind you that Christian faith is still the vital ingredient in an intimate relationship filled with true love and honest devotion.

Sign up today to receive your first set. Send no money now. We'll bill you only $9.97 post-paid with your shipment. Then every month you'll automatically receive the latest four "hot off the press" titles for the same low post-paid price of $9.97. That's a savings of 50% off the $4.95 cover price. When you consider the exaggerated shipping charges of other book clubs, your savings are even greater!

**THERE IS NO RISK**—you may cancel at any time without obligation. And if you aren't completely satisfied with any selection, return it for an immediate refund.

**TO JOIN,** just complete the coupon below, mail it today, and get ready for hours of wholesome entertainment.

Now you can curl up, relax, and enjoy some great reading full of the warmhearted spirit of romance.